FORGIVE ME, NADIA

VERONIKA GASPARYAN

Forgive Me, Nadia

A Thrilling Novel Filled with Love, Pain, Captivity, and

an Ultimate Test of One's Faith.

by

Veronika Gasparyan

Forgive Me, Nadia

Visit author's website at www.VeronikaGasparyan.com for more information.

First Edition

ISBN-13: 978-0-692-93149-3

Written by Veronika Gasparyan

Cover Design by Zoella Rose Designs

Edited by Mary Ring

Parts of the story contributed by the published author, Dr. Tigran Kazaryan

NOTE TO THE READER

This book is a work of fiction based on a true story. Names, characters, places, and incidents either are the product of the author's imagination or are used in a fictitious manner. Any resemblance to actual persons living or dead, events or locations is entirely coincidental.

DEDICATION

To all those children who are struggling to survive and are held captive within the sex-trafficking world full of criminals, pedophiles, and corrupted politicians. If you have a chance to read this book and have been affected by the human-trafficking issue in one way or another, please know that you are not alone. There are millions of children and young adults just like you all around the world who are abused and emotionally hurt. Please try your best to escape from the situation you are in or at least stay strong and do not lose your faith. One strong boy wisely wrote,

"An unbreakable mind is a key to an indestructible body."

"Sometimes, respect from others is earned not by creating fear, but by forgiving them their sins."

Veronika Gasparyan

FORGIVE ME,

NADIA

CHAPTER ONE

In the heartless yet beautiful city of Moscow, scared and in pain Natalia lay on her bed. She was barely 17. It was May 1st, but the poor girl had lost track of days a while back. The only thing she could guess at that moment was the time - one o'clock in the morning. That's when her regular workdays usually ended.

This night was different. A few minutes ago, one of the pimps let in an unexpected client. Some influential politician who was apparently too horny to fall sleep.

The bedroom, which was the only room she had lived in for the past few months, was medium in size but at least 18 feet by 12 feet. It was considered the most sizable bedroom in the building, at least per the old Soviet Union standards. There was a window on the wall across the entrance, but it was boarded up from the inside way before Natalia got there. Overall the whole building and the rooms were not well-kept.

Faded floral wallpaper was peeling off of the walls. The uneven floor, once covered with beautiful hardwood, was now rotten, stained and dirty. The ceiling, which was white when they built the house, was now beige with yellow watermarks all over it. On top of all that, the smoking of cigarettes, which the clients were allowed to do, made the smell and overall appearance of the bedroom look like yellow–tinted fog.

If the terrible interior were not enough, the bedroom had a smell of rotten leftovers, mostly from the contents of the open and expired cans that were given to Natalia daily. All that was also mixed with the scent of half-eaten boiled eggs, some unfinished meat and other leftovers that she couldn't force herself to eat. In addition to canned food Natalia was given a regular cooked food once a week, usually after a party that the pimps would have in one of the other rooms.

When it came to liquids, Natalia got a metal bucket filled with faucet water every Monday morning. Occasionally, she also got a plastic cup filled with milk, but half of the time the milk was already spoiled and to disgusting to drink.

If all that was not enough to fill the room with an awful odor, there was a red bucket placed in one of the corners. It was half full of Natalia's urine and feces. The smell was appalling, and despite complaints from the customers, the room was not cleaned from that often enough. The leftovers were removed once or twice per month, and her bucket was emptied one day a week when they dropped off the fresh water. It was shocking how anyone could voluntarily walk into that room and stay there for more than a few seconds, never mind having sex.

Despite all those inhumane conditions, Natalia's unexpected client was apparently not disgusted enough to leave. He was in his early sixties and dressed professionally. He looked like someone who had just finished a business meeting; yet, his pants were unzipped and halfway down his legs. He was standing right next to her bed, giving her a dirty, disgusted look. Expected by him, Natalia's service was not going to happen. That was obvious. By now, Natalia was in too much pain, moaning louder and louder.

"I am NOT wasting any more time. I am calling Ivan!" said the politician. A second later he pulled out his cell phone and dialed out. Ivan was the chief pimp for the whole neighborhood and happened to manage that location personally.

"Ivan! This bitch is playing hard to get. I don't have time for this, and she is killing my mood! Come here and take care of this right now!" He slammed the flip-phone closed and stuck it back in his pocket. Meanwhile, with pain increasing by the minute, Natalia started to panic. The moment the door lock turned, she covered herself with the ripped-up blanket and curled into a ball.

When Ivan walked in, the politician turned towards him and immediately walked over, throwing his hands up in the air. It was apparent that despite Natalia's condition, and because he had already paid for her services, he was still planning on getting his due.

"What do you think you are doing, you stupid whore?" screamed Ivan as he came up to her bed. "Do you want to get beat up as you did three months ago? Don't you know what happens when whores like you piss off our best clients?"

"Do you have any other pregnant girls in here?" asked the impatient politician, grabbing his pants in case the answer was no.

"We have one," said Ivan, "but she is only four months along and very skinny. Let's go outside and talk. This place

5

stinks like shit."

When they left the room, and the door lock turned, Natalia moved to the middle of the bed and spread her legs wide open. Her body was naturally guiding her through active labor. She wanted to scream from intense pain but was too scared.

Before she could think about what to do next, she realized that the baby was about to come out. She started to push to the best of her abilities and count out loud. It seemed to help her during the labor.

"Oneee . . . Twooo . . . Threee . . . Oh God, help me! Four . . . Fiiiiive."

A minute later, a little, miniature head showed up between her legs. The baby's head was now fully visible. Natalia was overwhelmed. She gently grabbed the baby by the neck and with another push, pulled the rest of the baby out. It seemed like she somehow knew what to do: just one of the wonders of Mother Nature.

She gently grabbed the newborn and started to clean its face and head as fast as she could. The realization that she, herself had just become a mother, had not hit her yet.

A few seconds later, after the baby's face was nice and clean, Natalia abruptly stopped, looked at the newborn and tears started to flow down her face. She had a little angel in her hands. It was hers. She created it.

If any sadness about the predicament she had been in was filling up her heart, it was all gone now. What she had now was an unexplainable motherly joy: a feeling she had never imagined. Her slowly developing bond with the baby during the pregnancy was different from holding the child in her hands. The love was purely overflowing from her body and into her priceless little miracle. The baby looked just like her, and just like her, it was a beautiful little girl. Although it was only a few minutes ago that the baby was born, it felt to Natalia, like time had stopped. She knew, however, that she still had a lot to do.

The baby had not cried yet, and Natalia recalled hearing that newborns have to make noises so they can clear their lungs. She had witnessed a few house-births in the place where she grew up. Nurses used to turn babies upside down and gently strike their butts. That way babies would react and make sounds.

Without thinking about it much longer, she grabbed her baby girl by the feet and turned her upside down. It wasn't easy because the umbilical cord was still attached to the placenta which Natalia's body had not yet expelled. She had to do this, so with a gentle force, she lightly slapped the baby's bottom. A few seconds later, she heard her infant's first cry.

She put the baby down, afraid that Ivan was going to come back in at any minute. Collecting whatever strength she had left, she pulled at the umbilical cord, and finally, the placenta came out. The little girl was lying between her mother's legs and was still making distressed but full-of-life sounds.

The moment Natalia pulled the mass out, she heard fast-approaching footsteps in the corridor. She quickly wrapped the placenta and the baby in her thin blanket as Ivan walked in. Natalia was scared - very scared - but the beautiful face of her daughter kept her calm. She felt like she was staring into a mirror from the past. For the first time in many years, Natalia's still youthful face was displaying a truly genuine smile. Finally, she had someone else in her life: God's gift for all the struggles she had endured.

"What the hell?" screamed Ivan, in total shock. "What is this? Oh, God, what am I going to do now? It was not supposed to happen for at least another month!" He sounded confused and lost. That baby must have been the first one that was born in this organization. The first mistake they made, and it was on his watch.

He nervously grabbed his cell phone and dialed out. His hand was shaking, a strange thing to see in a grown man. "Madam Liz? It's Ivan from the 13th location. We have a huge problem. I don't even know how to tell you this. We-we-we have a newborn here," he stuttered. "It wasn't supposed to happen for another month, and we were going to shoot the bitch two weeks from now, but here I am. I don't know what to do. Can you please…?"

Madam Liz must have hung up on him because he closed his flip phone in a rush, way before he could finish what he was saying. Madam Liz oversaw the physical conditions of the working girls, not only for the city of Moscow but also for the whole region. Judging by her actions, she was in a respected position. Natalia had never met her, but that's because Ivan and a few of the other local pimps kept her pregnancy a secret. They wanted to make some extra bucks without giving all of it to their bosses.

There had always been a particular clientele who desired expecting girls: the bigger the belly, the better. There were all types of perverted guys from different backgrounds and age groups, who paid double and triple to have sex with a pregnant girl, not to mention sex with a gorgeous one.

Natalia was not average looking, by far. She was taller than the others, proportionally built, and had straight, long blond hair, big beautiful eyes and was someone you might see on the cover of a fashion magazine. She always made the pimps a lot of money and when she got pregnant, and her belly started to show, Ivan just could not make himself do what he was supposed to do. He was supposed to take her for a two-hour ride and shoot her quietly in the outskirts of the city. The constant flow of customers and cash made Ivan lose track of time, and now he had gotten himself into a dangerous mess.

Meanwhile, Natalia cleaned up her little girl's body and re-wrapped her tighter in the blanket. She used extra material to put in between the baby and placenta so the newborn would be comfortable and clean.

"Hey, little girl! I know you are hungry," she said to her daughter. Natalia's voice was full of love and care. The baby was desperately sucking on her thumb. Natalia had the food ready to go. She pulled up her T-shirt, and gently placed her nipple into the baby's mouth. Her daughter started to suck on her mother's breast trying to get every drop of milk she could.

At first, Natalia felt uncomfortable and in pain but the little one quickly got into a rhythm, and a few moments later the process became effortless for both. Breastfeeding her baby became an experience that she could not describe in words. She felt empowered and vital in giving her child something essential, something irreplaceable by anything in the world, something extraordinary.

As the baby got into the rhythm of eating, Natalia's tension eased up, and she just watched, in complete silence. The little girl was looking straight into her mother's eyes with pure love. She looked just like Natalia when she was born. And she had the same blue eyes, like a bright summer sky. The mother and child were bonding at the speed of light.

The whole time Natalia was feeding her baby, Ivan was by

the door, pacing back and forth. About 20 minutes after his call, the door opened, and Madam Liz walked in. The moment she was inside, the whole room filled up with a mix of different types of perfume. It was an overpowering smell, but it was better than what was in the place until then.

Madam Liz was a lovely woman in her early fifties. Her shiny black hair was up and held nicely with a unique vintage barrette. Tastefully done makeup was covering her perfect classic features. Her exclusive designer dress with a belt made of crystals, lay perfectly flat on her hips, making her bottle-shaped figure even more noticeable. She had on a sophisticated outfit flawlessly matched with an animal print clutch and high heel boots that she wore with much self-assurance. Although she was in a rush to get there, she looked like she had spent a long time getting ready. It would have taken a regular woman at least three hours to look even remotely close to how she looked. With her neck and hands covered in gold and diamonds and the way she carried herself, it was clear that Madam Liz was powerful and rich.

She walked right by Ivan, purposely making loud noises with her boots. She didn't even look at him. It was obvious she was pissed. On the other hand, Ivan was so scared that he took a step back as she passed by him. He could sense her anger and threatening manner.

The bed sheet under Natalia was dirty and had all sorts of liquids on it, from her earlier delivery. It grossed Madam Liz out, and she kept her distance from the young family by at least 3 feet. She gave Natalia a dirty, degrading look and their eyes met for a split second. That was more than enough for the young mother to show to Madam how much pain and suffering she was feeling.

All that Natalia saw staring back at her though were dark

anger-filled eyes. Madam's lips were tense with a little twitching. They matched her raging, heartless demeanor. She looked like she could have a nervous breakdown at any second.

The older woman broke the silence with a surprisingly calm voice. "This is happening in such horrible timing! It's the worst thing this house has ever seen!"

Natalia was already looking down, not knowing what to do or what to say. When she didn't hear Madam say anything else, she decided to look up and face the woman and whatever else fate had in store for her.

Their eyes met once again, but this time Natalia was trying to talk to Madam Liz silently and somehow convince her to have some mercy. The young girl was genuinely hoping that somewhere deep within those dark, angry eyes there was light. After all, Madam was also a woman, and maybe she was even a mother. Perhaps there was still something human there, hiding quietly in her soul under all that makeup and hatred.

"I named her Nadia. It's short for Nadejda, which means hope," said Natalia with a sad, yet genuine smile. She never had a typical mother. Her birth mother never took good care of her. She had spent most of her youth in the neighbors' houses, while her parents were getting drunk, already asleep at home or on one of the park benches. For a moment, Natalia wished that Madam was her mother and the three-year-long nightmare was now over. The reaction she got back was not what she expected. The woman made an angry, infuriated face and rapidly turned around, walking quickly towards Ivan.

"How many times do I have to say that pregnant whores HAVE to go as soon as their bellies show? Ten times? Twenty times? Thirty times? How many times did I tell you that sooner or later your money-hungry ass will get us all in trouble?" Her voice was rising higher and higher. Her face was now closer to his. She was getting on her tippy toes to match his height like he was some troubled boy and she was a nun in the Catholic school.

"I know! I know! I'm sorry, Madam. I don't know what came over me and the others. She always made us tons of money, and we didn't want to let her go." His head was down, and he spoke in an almost inaudible whisper. It was nothing like Natalia had seen before. The bad-ass pimp was now a little punk kid, scared and frightened for his life.

"How am I going to explain this to our bosses? Tell me! I don't even know what they would do to you! I cannot even imagine, but, you can explain to them what happened yourself. I'm staying out of it! Let's go!"

"Madam, what do I do with these two?" he asked meekly.

"Give her a can of soup and lock them in. We'll be back tomorrow to take care of it. Now let's go!" she answered. Ivan opened a can of chicken soup and placed it on the floor next to the bed. Without saying a word, he and Madam Liz walked out and locked the door on Natalia and the baby.

The young mother felt at ease as soon as they left. She decided to clean up the mess and finish taking care of the baby. One thing that had to be taken care of was the umbilical cord, which was still attached to the baby. She had to find a way to cut it, but there wasn't anything in that room that she could use. She hadn't seen utensils in months.

Natalia decided to bite right through it and carefully placed the baby and the placenta on the bed. She gave the room one more glance and right before biting down on the cord she noticed the metal can of soup that Ivan opened. Happy that she didn't have to bite down on something that just came out of her, she grabbed the sharp, still-attached lid and used it to cut the umbilical cord. There wasn't much blood, and Natalia did her best at tying a knot with the end that was still attached to her newborn. She pulled the wet sheet from under herself and found a dry spot on the mattress to lie on, for her and the baby. Tired and weak, the young family finally drifted off to sleep - two little girls – awaiting their unfair destiny to unfold.

Around 10 o'clock the next night, the door opened, and Madam Liz walked in with another man. He was in his mid-forties and someone Natalia hadn't seen before. Ivan was not with them. His luck must have run out, and his body was probably somewhere far away from the city, lying lifelessly where Natalia's body could have been.

The new man looked very professional, wearing a perfectly pressed black suit, red tie, and white button-down shirt sticking out stylishly from under the jacket. His cologne was strong but sensual. His short dark hair was perfectly spiked above his smooth hairline and nicely shaped forehead. The reserved look in his eyes made him look very attractive. For a moment Natalia thought that he and Madam Liz were a couple, but then she reasoned that who knew what his real role was. There was nothing friendly about him.

Natalia was sitting in the middle of the bed, holding her baby and staring at him. He gave her a brief, empty glance and looked back at Madam. She looked back at him, and in a strange, almost imperceptible manner, they had a swift, silent conversation. The man shook his head, and Madam Liz turned to look at Natalia.

The young mother shifted to the edge of the bed, holding her little bundle of joy that she grew to love so much and so fast. The baby was triple-wrapped in the blanket. That was the only piece of material Natalia could use. The bed sheet was on the floor and mostly wet. No one had washed it yet since she first arrived at that location.

During the past three months, the poor girl had at least 100 clients a week, which probably amounted to over 400 per month. From the countless amounts of their fluids and all the blood and liquids from the delivery, that sheet was utterly unusable. Up until yesterday, it was hard and dry from her client's bodily discharges drying out on it, layer upon layer. To be able to lie on it and even sleep, she would think of the days when she used to rest on the dry hay in a barn in her village. That's where she used to take afternoon naps during the summer months.

"Listen to me, you stupid teen," said Madam Liz. "We have to get rid of your bastard as soon as possible! Do you understand me; as soon as possible?"

"What do you mean Madam?" asked Natalia. Her eyes filled with tears and her whole body shook. "I don't want to give my baby to the orphanage. Please! That's my baby!"

"The orphanage? What orphanage? Are you out of your mind? Has too much fucking around got into your head? You have no documents and who would be so stupid as to drop that thing off there? What if we get caught? Are you trying to bring the whole organization down?"

The man, whose name was unknown, was still standing by the door, quietly observing what was going on. He had no emotions on his face. The only time he moved was to lift his right sleeve and check the time on his shiny, expensive-looking gold watch.

"Here is what we are going to do," said Madam. "Either you choke your kid right here and wrap it in a plastic bag or keep it alive and we will throw it into the dumpster ourselves! It is completely up to you, but you need to decide right now!"

Natalia looked at her in disbelief. Her eyes were wide with terror. Her trembling lips opened like she was about to take her last breath. What she heard made her motherly instincts burst right through her ribcage. Her conscious mind no longer controlled her obedient nature. Like a prisoner who was given the last wish before the execution, she screamed out in unstoppable passion.

"Oh! My God! No! Please! Madam Liz! Don't kill my baby! I will do whatever it takes to keep her alive! I will fuck more clients. I will clean this whole house and other locations if you want! I can even take care of more babies from other girls!" begged Natalia. Her whole face was red, and tears streamed from her eyes.

"Listen to me, you stupid whore! There are no other bastards! Just yours! We haven't kept pregnant whores alive for over a year! You will co-operate and let us throw away your "garbage"! If not, then both of you will be sliced up and thrown into the Moscow River, like the others! Do you understand?"

The man in black still had zero emotions, and he was looking around the room in disgust. Madam turned to him and shook her head from side to side. He looked up at the ceiling, took a deep breath and started to walk towards Natalia, pulling out a pair of black rubber gloves from his pants pocket.

CHAPTER TWO

Sitting on the edge of her bed, Natalia squeezed little Nadia closer. The new mother was scared but still had her protective motherly instinct kicking in. The man slowly put on his black rubber gloves and looked at Natalia. She knew that he was coming for her little girl. He was going to kill her, if not both of them. Her short life, full of painful memories started to flash in front of her as if someone had pressed the fast-forward button on a DVD player.

A mix of memories filled up her mind. One was of the warm chicken soup her mother used to make when she was younger. Another one was the long summer days she spent with the other kids from her village, running around the green fields and picking ripe berries. Also, one of her favorite memories was the stories her friend's mom used to read to all the neighborhood girls, as they shared a huge, warm blanket by the bonfire on chilly spring nights. Then there was a quick but odd memory of a happy smile on her mother's face on Natalia's 10th birthday when her father brought home three bottles of vodka instead of the birthday cake.

That last memory snapped Natalia back into reality. She moved up to the headboard of the bed and covered Nadia with her arms in a protective manner. "I can't kill my baby girl! Please, Madam Liz! I can't!"

"Enough! You don't have to! I will do it for you! Give me that thing of yours, now!" said Madam Liz with aggravation. She took a big step towards the bed and made a motion to grab the child.

"No!" Natalia started screaming and crawled even further up the bed, away from Madam.

"My patience is running very low," the furious Madam said in a threatening voice. She then came up to the edge of the bed, bent down and slapped the shocked Natalia across the face. "You have five seconds to give her to me, or you both die!"

"Please! No! Don't you have a heart?"

"Five . . . Four . . . Threeee . . ."

"Ok, ok, ok, stop, just stop. Can I at least have ten more minutes? Please?" Natalia begged.

"No! You can't! You had the whole day, and by the way, what kind of stupid name is that? Why would you call her Hope, when the only hope you have right now is to smarten up and stay alive?"

A second later, Madam grabbed the baby's feet and started to pull her out of Natalia's arms. Nadia began to make an ear-piercing noise, crying as hard as her little lungs would let her. The young mother, realizing that her daughter was hurting, made the most difficult decision any reasonable mother would make.

"Wait! Please! Just wait! I made my choice. I pick the dumpster! I will co-operate," Natalia screamed out heartbreakingly and placed a loving, tearful kiss on her daughter's crying face.

The Madam let go of the baby, and composing herself, took a couple of steps back. "What a stupid generation! They only understand violence! Keep your fucking voice down! Between your screaming and that little shit crying, I am getting aggravated and short-fused! It's the third floor! The last thing I need is for someone to hear you." Madam Liz did not look beautiful to Natalia any longer. All she saw was darkness and hate written all over the woman's face.

Natalia fixed up the blanket Nadia was wrapped in and started to rock the baby. The poor little thing was hungry. The young mother quickly figured out what she had to do and pulled up her shirt to breastfeed her baby. Nadia started to desperately drink any milk she could get out of her malnourished mother. "It's going to be ok my little angel; everything will be ok," said Natalia, hoping that everything was going to work out just right.

A minute later the exhausted baby fell asleep, and Natalia looked up at Madam in hopes of a miracle. She still could not believe that all this was happening. Tears were streaming down her face and onto Nadia's blanket. It was a sad scene, but Madam Liz was not moved by it at all. The heartless Madam still had an entirely lifeless expression on her face. It was questionable whether she was even capable of any emotion and if she was a human being in the first place.

All the Madam did is adjust her clothes and pat her hair, while making annoyed and exasperated sounds. "This is insane! I had to get physical with some trash!" she snapped just loudly enough for the young mother to hear.

Natalia was a very obedient type; but since becoming a mother, she acquired some extra power that she never had before. She had always been different from the rest and rarely spoke about her life or feelings. From the beginning, Natalia had found the way to be at peace even during her unfortunate predicament. Natalia believed that it was her destiny and there wasn't much she could do about it. She had no identity, no papers and nowhere to go.

"Ok, give the baby to me now. We will keep it in the car and throw it away before sunrise," said Madam, in a calmer voice.

Natalia's heart was pounding. Her whole body was in pain, as she contemplated separation from her daughter: the only person she loved. She was not ready to let go and was never going to be.

Without thinking much longer, she got off the bed and with Nadia still in her arms, dropped down to her knees. Something pushed her to beg Madam Liz to spare little Nadia's life.

"Please! Please let me throw my baby away myself!" Her voice was low and pleading. Her head was bowed down. Madam's expensive patent leather boots caught her eyes, and for a moment she could see her reflection in them. "I just want to be with her a little more. I promise I will do it. I will throw her out with my own hands. That's my wish. Please!"

She covered her wet face with the palm of her hand and started to cry. She wasn't loud, but her cry was soul-wrenching. It was now up to Madam Liz, whether to bring the newborn to the dumpster herself or let Natalia do it.

After not hearing any response back from the woman, Natalia stopped, took a deep breath, and looked up. She felt that she needed to say something else: something that could appeal to the Madam even more.

"I can stay in the back seat and keep the baby quiet until we arrive. I promise I will not try to run or do anything stupid. I will make sure that your ride is as smooth as it can be."

"Are you crazy? Sitting on your bloody ass in the back seat of our brand new BMW?" Madam laughed. "Do you think we are fools? We are the furthest from it; plus, what the hell are you trying to say? You were begging me not to kill your offspring just a few minutes ago, and now you are begging us to let you throw her out yourself! What a great mother YOU are," she added with sarcasm. It was apparent she enjoyed seeing Natalia in this condition; crying, begging, and hurting.

The poor girl didn't say anything. She just prayed that by some miracle her luck would turn around and she would be able to spend a little more time with her daughter. She was well-aware of how outrageous her request sounded, but that was the best choice she had out of all of the despicable and inhumane options. Now she knew why so many times, while growing up, she heard disturbing news on TV, reporting: "Another newborn was found this morning dead in the dumpster."

"Here is what we are going to do," said Madam. "We'll be back at 3 a.m. I hope you appreciate this and will show me your gratefulness for letting you spend more time with your thing!"

Natalia shook her head yes, without saying anything else and stayed on the floor until Madame Liz and the man left the room. It was still unclear what exact role that man played and why he was silently standing near the door the whole time. She guessed that he was probably a killer and the woman brought him along in case Natalia put up a fight or tried to escape.

With only a few hours left together, Natalia got back up on the bed and laid little Nadia down right next to her. While she was pregnant, she sang different lullabies out loud, especially during those few minutes in between her clients. While Nadia was in her mother's womb, Natalia's singing seemed to calm her down. Natalia remembered a few melodies from the times she spent at her neighbor's house, but she improvised the words on her own.

In a quiet and loving voice, Natalia started to sing.

> *Baiu Baiushki Baiu,*
> *Little Baby, I love you.*
> *Even puppy, bird, and cat.*
> *All are here by your bed.*
> *They are all singing songs like these.*
> *Rocking Nadia into dreams.*

.   .   .

The loud voice, right over her face, woke her up. "Get up you stupid bitch! I told you to be ready by 3 a.m.! Let's go!" screamed Madam Liz into Natalia's face.

"I'm very sorry. I fell asleep while singing to my baby. I am ready. Look, I'm already up."

"I don't care! Sing to Satan himself but be ready when I tell you to be! Don't forget I am doing YOU a huge favor! Wrap that thing up and let's go! Oh, and you are not coming back here after we dump your garbage. You will get cleaned up and groomed, then moved to a new location: much more upscale and for wealthy clientele only. Many men waited all these months for you to recover. They are interested in renting you out for a week, a month, or even longer. You can thank me later! Now, let's go!"

Natalia got off the bed, quickly ripped off a small piece of the peeling wallpaper and started to press down on it with her long, broken fingernails. "N A D I A," she wrote and tucked it in between the folds of Nadia's blanket.

The door was unlocked and wide open. Madam Liz was

already in the hallway along with the man, waiting for her to come out. Natalia took a few steps towards the door, then turned around and stopped. She glanced up and down the room, from wall to wall, and then at her bed. Yes, it was the worst and the longest time she had ever been locked up; at the same time, it was a safe zone that made her feel familiar and content.

Out of nowhere, she got an urge to do something childish. Despite her troubled life, Natalia was still a young girl, so she rushed towards the red bucket that was her toilet, and kicked it with her bare foot, as hard as she could. The contents spilled all over the floor, and she couldn't help but laugh at it in a genuinely happy manner. It felt good to do something out of her character, something "bad."

She walked out of her room and headed down the stairs, pressing little Nadia's face into her chest. Madam Liz and the man were a few steps ahead of Natalia, and she tried to keep up the pace without paying any attention to the inside of the house. She had never heard voices of other girls there and only knew of dinners the pimps had every couple of weeks. At this point, it didn't matter. It was in the past, and she just wanted to get out of there, even without knowing how the night was going to end.

The moment her feet stepped onto the sidewalk, she looked up. She hadn't seen morning or night sky in over seven months. It was dark, with millions of stars; some brighter than others.

She looked down at the baby and saw Nadia's eyes wide open. It seemed like the little girl was enjoying the fresh air and the magical night sky as much as her mother was. Natalia knew that this was one of the last few memories they were going to experience together. It made her feel sad and disappointed, yet happy to have the opportunity to have this memory.

Before the little girl was born, Natalia planned all kinds of things that she wanted them to do together, like going clothes shopping, braiding her hair, painting her nails, and even taking a nap on that dry summer hay in the barn of her village.

Natalia turned her head to the right and saw the black BMW sedan with the trunk wide open. It was parked a few feet away from her, but near enough to see that Madam Liz was already sitting on the front passenger side. The man was still outside, standing by the trunk, looking right at Natalia.

His presence, both the night before and that moment, made Natalia feel very uncomfortable. Even though he hadn't said a word, it was just the way he carried himself, his clothes, and that empty look in his eyes that made her feel tense. The black rubber gloves he was wearing also added to the creepy vibes he was giving out. The man pointed to the open trunk. It was clear that if she didn't get in right away, he would force her in there himself.

Natalia walked over and carefully climbed in. It wasn't easy, both physically and emotionally. She was holding on to the baby with both of her hands, and on top of it, she had always been afraid of the darkness. Natalia's mother made her stay in a dark closet when other alcoholics came over to get drunk. Since then, small spaces without lights always triggered anxiety. Knowing she had no other choice, Natalia concentrated her thoughts and got into the trunk, lying right down and placing Nadia in front of her, facing each other.

The man shut the trunk and walked away, leaving the young and innocent family trying to make the best out of this terrible situation. It was dark, but the bright moon seemed to be on their side. The beams were sinking right through every possible space they could find, easing Natalia's tension.

The car moved and then quickly sped up to a steady pace. The smell in the trunk was surprisingly pleasant. It reminded

Natalia of strawberry fields she used to run through, berry picking and lying in the fresh green grass; something she would love to do with her daughter one day. All she wanted was to feel like she had a real family for once.

They had a long, two-hour trip ahead of them. A few minutes later, Nadia drifted off to sleep. For Natalia, sleeping was an impossible option. She had way too much on her mind. Wide awake, she started to think about her life; about the things she had seen. She wondered how all of that came to this very moment; in this trunk with her newborn, forced by evil beings to commit a terrible crime.

The day before she turned fourteen, was the last time Natalia saw both of her parents. She still remembered that day vividly. They were talking to each other in the kitchen and then moved to the bedroom when Natalia got home. After discussing something for a little while, her mother called someone on the phone. She was nervous and rambling. Natalia could not make out through the closed door, what her mother was saying or who she was talking to and couldn't see much through the small, old-fashioned keyhole. All she knew was that about four hours after that phone call, three men came walking into their kitchen. They came for her.

Natalia's long-term alcoholic parents ended up selling her to a so-called organization. Its primary purpose was sex trafficking of underage girls. The group operated all over the world with its most prominent concentration in Europe and Russia.

What was the price the organization paid for Natalia? It was Stolichnaya Vodka: a whole ten bottles of it! The sale price for the poor girl was the topic of conversation in that discussion her mother had over the phone. How they got in touch with those men was unknown, but when you are an addict of any kind, you will find where the bad guys are, one way or another.

Natalia remembered one of the men holding the large case with vodka bottles and her parents rushing to get it as fast as they could. She recalled two men grabbed her, covering her mouth with tape and tying her hands behind her back. Then there was a quick sharp needle in her neck with drugs to put her to sleep. She woke up the next morning in the basement of some building, with dozens of young girls crying and asking for their parents. That day she turned fourteen years old.

Her "birthday gift" from the organization was a three-hour dolling-up session. They shaved her legs, armpits, and pubic area, changing her hair from straight to wavy and covering her face with thick makeup, making her look 30, not 14. After all that, they dressed her up in lace lingerie and brought her to the farthest part of the basement. The thick cement wall and a triple metal door separated it from the rest. There, a couple of older women gave her a last head-to-toe checkup and pushed her onto a small stage with lots of bright lights which were beaming right on her.

She could not recall much more from that night because she was drugged just like all the other girls who were there. She did remember though, seeing at least a couple of dozen men of all ages, sizes, and looks, sitting at small round tables, drinking expensive liquor and smoking thick cigars.

Auctioning off her virginity only took 5 minutes. Her body went to the highest bidder for 1000 US dollars. He was an old, heavyset man from Afghanistan, who spent money primarily on virgin girls under the age of eighteen: the younger, the better.

All the other details from her 14th birthday she buried deep inside and had no desire in digging them out. A few days after that night, she was on the streets of Moscow, alongside other girls, where her somewhat normal life stopped, and her mere existence began.

Two and a half years later, when she threw up for the first time early in the morning, was the last day she worked the streets. That morning one of the pimps took her for a checkup by the organization's head physician.

She recalled that day precisely because it was one of the coldest Decembers Moscow had seen in years. Thermometer readings, even during the day, fell twenty degrees below zero Fahrenheit. Snow was everywhere. The sidewalks covered in dirty snow drifts, left no room for the girls to stand on. They were all forced to walk the main roads and endanger their lives with cars being driven recklessly on the icy streets.

Natalia was always amazed that even in that type of weather, the business never stopped. Hot, cold, raining, or snowing - there were still cars and SUVs pulling up and away, up and away. Sometimes, they would circle the streets for a few minutes before finally stopping. They were merely searching for the best looking prostitute available for a pick-up.

Most of those cars had tinted windows, and you couldn't even see who was inside, not that it mattered. They were just a bunch of hungry animals, hunting for their prey, picking up broken down souls: the beautiful and young fairies of the night.

Natalia was rarely available. She was the most beautiful and one of the youngest girls in the region. Many times a car would already be waiting for her before she got dropped off by another client. She would just come out of one car and right into the next. If she were lucky enough, there would already be another girl or two in the back seat. That would mean less work for her and usually a safer environment. Then the car would disappear into the mysterious night, and another chapter of her story would be born.

Pimps, or better-said criminals, collected the cash. US dollars were the most preferred method of payment. The clientele didn't care about the age of the working girls. The younger ones were usually the most popular because they were in better shape and better kept-up than the others.

That particular branch of the organization controlled the central metropolitan area, which covered a section of about ten square miles. Most nights there would be around 100 girls working throughout the center of the city, but there were a lot more than that. About 200 more were locked up inside houses called brothels and drugged so they wouldn't leave. Most of the girls there were either too old, too sick, or just didn't behave well enough and gave pimps and clients on the streets too much trouble.

Another reason the brothels were useful was that some of the clients were either too well known to take a chance and be seen or just too shy to approach working girls on the street. For them, to make their desire a reality and in a more comfortable setting, brothels were the best option. What they didn't know before they went there was that most of those properties hadn't seen a makeover since the construction, many decades back. Not that the men with such low morals would even care about it, but still.

In some strange way, Natalia preferred working the streets instead of being locked up in the building. She heard from others that the girls working indoors were forced to take a massive dose of drugs to keep them subdued. Some of her clients talked at the parties and referred to the drugged ones as lifeless dolls.

At least two to three girls would die each month from an overdose and their bodies would never be found. The organization employed many killers. They did their job very well and left the victims in pieces, in many locations.

If not for overdose, then another reason for the working girls to be killed, was their pregnancies. No one knew when or how they died because as soon as the test that the ex-con physician gave them came back positive, the girls disappeared. The so-called doctor was hired by the organization after he lost his license due to malpractice. He served ten years in prison and then got recruited by bosses and offered a job. He was the one to administer the pregnancy test and then estimate how far along the girls were. The pimps and killers handled the rest.

On an infrequent occasion, if the pregnant prostitutes were pretty and popular among the clients, the pimps would vote on letting them live, at least until the beginning of the last trimester. It hadn't happened in a long time, but that exception to the rule did exist. Natalia ended up being the one.

Mother Nature was kind and generous to her. She gifted Natalia with way-above-average looks. She was not just cute; she was beautiful and perfect in every way. She was taller than the others, proportionally built, and had straight, blond hair, nicely falling to her small waist. The long black eyelashes emphasized her big blue eyes. She had a natural look that you would only see on the cover of a fashion magazine. She looked better than most professional models after they spend a full day of make-overs to look perfect. If someone from Hollywood had only known about Natalia, she could have been a supermodel instead of a teenager forced into prostitution at age 14.

She was by far one of the most valuable possessions the organization had. Men used to come from all over the region just to fuck her. They paid more than double for her in comparison to other girls. Her clients came from many professions and backgrounds. They ranged from young school teachers, construction workers, cops, and firefighters, to professors, pilots, people in business and politicians. Even the poor college students of the nearby universities knew about her and saved their money for months just to buy her for 10-15 minutes. Between her looks and obedient personality, she made everyone prosperous and happy. Killing her right away made no sense.

That same night when Natalia got sick, and the pimps took her to see that doctor, was when she first learned about her pregnancy. From there, they moved her to the same location where she lived for the next seven months.

The room where they had brought her was dirty and old right from the start, but still, it was a bedroom. She was nervous but again behaved so that the pimps wouldn't drug her. She listened to whatever they told her to do. At that time she didn't yet know that selling her body on cold streets of Moscow was better than being used non-stop all day long by hundreds of men. To top it all off she had no other girls to talk to, no breaks in between, no fresh air, and zero freedom.

At the beginning of her time in that house, she had a different pimp, not Ivan. His name was Max. He was tall, heavy-set, mean, and always screamed at everybody. He only let her clean up a couple of times per month and did that in a very degrading manner. He would bring her to the nonfunctioning area of the house that used to be a bathroom and tell her to get naked. When she did, he would use the hose to wash her down with cold water for a minute straight. He didn't care that she was an expecting mother and had a belly.

When he got transferred, Natalia was beyond happy. Any pimp other than Max was better for her; so, when Ivan arrived she was relieved. He was skinny, not as tall as Max, didn't look that mean and got mad on infrequent occasions. He also let her wash-up on her own and in one of the bathrooms that had hot water. She felt safe living indoors under Ivan's supervision; although, there were things that she craved from working on the streets.

She missed beautiful sunrises, fresh winter air, and the smell of new flowers in the spring, the aroma of rose bushes during the summer and multi-colored trees in the fall. On a rare occasion, she was lucky enough, and a client would rent her for the whole night. When that happened, most of the time he would take her to a hotel or a fully-functioning apartment. There, she was able to eat real food and have a regular shower, as well as a nap for an hour or two. Interestingly enough, Natalia never tried to run away or steal from any of those clients, even though they were asleep in a few seconds after sex. It seemed that she had learned to find peace within her heart and live her life without fighting the reality of it.

Of course, the streets weren't always that safe. There were a few sick men whom she, unfortunately, had to serve. They abused her, tied her down, or had other types of sex with her that she didn't agree to or want. There wasn't much she could do. She was a sex slave, and there was no one in the world there for her. Other than letting her have a quick shower, Ivan kept Natalia locked in her bedroom 24/7. The reality of being a pregnant prostitute was much worse than Natalia had expected. Instead of her catching a break, they worked her much harder than before.

Though lucky for her, most of her current clients were either rich or didn't have much time on their hands. Some of them were in and out within 10-15 minutes, despite paying for half an hour. It was a big deal to Natalia to get those few extra minutes in between each of them. It made it a little easier. She was able to get up and stretch out or walk around the room instead of lying horizontally hour after hour. It was a fact that being pregnant made her profession much more challenging. The good thing was that most of her clients had never heard of

Kama Sutra and were not into trying different things in sex.

·　　·　　·

The BWM abruptly stopped, and Natalia instantly returned to reality. The baby was still sleeping. Madam Liz and the man got out of the car, and he opened the trunk. Madam Liz checked the area to make sure no one was there and looked at Natalia.

"Quick, let's go. Get out of the trunk," Madam said to Natalia. "This location is perfect," she said to the man.

Natalia slowly crawled out of the trunk holding onto little Nadia as tightly as she could. The baby wasn't even crying. Madam Liz pointed to the dark alley near the row of buildings and looked at Natalia. "You, walk toward those two metal dumpsters on the left and then do what we came here to do! Understand?"

Quietly and obediently Natalia nodded and pressed the baby close against her chest. She headed towards the dark alley, with the moonlight shining on her path. It felt like the moon was trying its best to stay in the sky long enough to watch over Natalia, but it had to go so that the sun could rise.

A couple of dozens of steps later, in the midst of early morning fog, she saw the silhouette of the two dumpsters Madam Liz described. They looked like two coffins at the cemetery. The first one had an open cover and reminded Natalia of an ancient dragon she saw in some children's books. The dragon had a big, open mouth waiting for someone to give him an offering.

The young mother was overwhelmed. She was finally getting a full grip on what she was about to do. She was nervous and distraught with sweat running down both sides of her forehead. It wasn't from being hot or overheated. She was cold from wearing thin clothes and standing outside in the fresh air of the early morning. She was sweating from being scared and afraid of it all.

With each step she took, frantic thoughts were filling up her mind. She wondered what would happen if she just started to run; run into that dark alley and keep moving until everyone else was far behind them. The man would surely try to shoot at her, but he could miss. What if she started to scream for help and by some miracle, someone heard it.

All those creative ideas got replaced the moment she approached the dumpsters. The realization that none of that was possible and both she and little Nadia were doomed took over. All of a sudden, the thought of the man killing them both, did not seem that bad of an idea. She preferred dying alongside her daughter anyway. At least she wouldn't be the one who left a child to a slow death inside a large metal dumpster, but none of that was in the plan that destiny had for the poor Natalia. It was not her time to die. It was just the first big test of faith.

"What, if by some miracle, someone finds you in time?" Natalia whispered in a comforting voice to her innocent and helpless daughter. "What if someone hears you cry and saves you?"

It sounded so promising and fortunate but at the same time very unrealistic and unlikely to happen. There was no one around, and the buildings in that alley seemed to be empty. It was apparent that Natalia still hadn't lost her naïve and pure hope in the miracles of life.

When she finally came up to the edge of the dumpster, she turned around and looked towards the car. Madam Liz and the man were both looking her way, and she saw him holding the long-barreled gun in his hands. He was pointing it straight towards Natalia. She knew that as soon as the baby was in the dumpster, she might get shot; although, if they were going to kill her, they would have done that by now. At this point, she didn't care. Meeting her daughter in heaven sounded better than continuing to live this way and alone.

She brought a child into this world and gave her life. Even if just for a day, it was still worth it. Despite being a young seventeen-year-old girl, she had a chance to feel what it was like to hold her flesh and blood in her hands. At least poor Natalia finally learned what unconditional love felt like, even in the midst of darkness and pain. Being a mother for a day was better than not being one at all.

With enormous hesitation, she got onto her tippy-toes and looked into the dumpster. It smelled awful and reminded her of the bedroom she had lived in for the past few months. She kissed her daughter's warm cheeks a dozen times and placed a last, loving kiss on her forehead. Little Nadia still wasn't crying. She felt safe in her mother's arms. Poor Natalia couldn't stop her tears from flowing. She looked for the garbage bag that was closest to the top of the dumpster, and gently placed her little girl on top of it.

"Be a good girl for mom and when I leave wait a few minutes and please start to cry as loud as you can. I love you with all my heart. You are my hope, my light, and my happiness. I will see you very soon. Mommy will be by your side forever and ever, and your guardian angels will watch over you until we meet again."

She turned towards the car with anger filling her from the inside out. In measured steps, she started to walk back towards the vehicle; at a steady pace at first, then faster and faster. As she got close enough for them to hear her, she started to repeat the same thing over and over again but louder each time.

"I am ready now! Go ahead! I am NOT afraid of you anymore!"

CHAPTER THREE

ll rise!" announced the bailiff in a loud and stern voice. Dozens of people all got up at once, and a second later the judge walked in. She was a woman with class and straight posture. Her brown hair was short and smooth and the high-end prescription glasses she had on, were sitting precisely on the tip of her small pointy nose. She seemed to represent herself as someone who was fair in her judgments. She sat down and immediately grabbed a thin, black folder prepared for her by the courtroom assistant.

"You may sit," the bailiff announced. "The court of Honorable Judge Medvedeva is now in session."

"Good afternoon, everyone," said the judge.

"Good afternoon, your honor," all replied.

"It's unnecessary to repeat today's calendar. We have only one more case to address," the judge said to the bailiff.

"We are going on record. Today is April 15th, 1991, and the

time is two o'clock in the afternoon. We are here for the sentencing of case Number 66-6933/1986 per Russian Federation Criminal Code 105 – Attempted first-degree murder of a newborn child, against Natalia Lebedeva, born April 1st, 1973. Are both parties ready?" asked the judge.

"Yes, your honor." answered the prosecutor.

"Yes, your honor," added the public defender.

The judge continued. "The defense has waived the right to a trial by jury and has given full power to this court to conduct a bench trial. A single judge will make the decision. In this case, it will be me, Supreme Court Judge Elena Medvedeva. Before the sentencing, all parties have a right to address the court one last time."

"We are ready," announced the prosecutor. His name was Mr. Chlenov, and just like the public defender, he was a recent graduate of a Moscow law school. If not for his perfectly-pressed gray suit, he would look like he was fifteen years old.

"Good morning, your honor! On May 3rd, 1990, at approximately 5 a.m. in the dumpster on Pushkin Street, Orekholo Region, a newborn was discovered in much distress, left in the metal garbage container to die. The child appeared alive but naked and wrapped in a dirty, wet blanket. A visual examination of the newborn revealed dangerously low vital signs. During the month-long trial that everyone can agree was fair, we heard the witness, who found the child, give his full statement. Furthermore, upon an examination of the newborn by the local emergency room pediatrician, the diagnoses were clear: frostbite, pneumonia, and slight hypothermia. The child had spent two weeks in the hospital and had made a full recovery since. She had been transferred into the state's care and assigned to a waiting list for adoption or available foster parents. Ms. Lebedeva could have brought her unwanted daughter to the church or an orphanage; but instead, she decided to throw her out, like a piece of garbage. God watched over this child, but so many newborns around the country aren't as lucky as she is. We, as conscientious citizens are responsible for teaching the younger generation a lesson. With that, the prosecution asks the court to sentence Ms. Lebedeva to the maximum allowed imprisonment of fifteen years. Thank you, your honor, the prosecution now rests."

Natalia was sitting in the front of the courtroom, locked up inside of the metal holding cage. She was just scared, quiet and stared at the floor. Meanwhile, every few minutes, people from the observing crowd shouted out derogatory names and phrases at her.

"Pig! Scumbag! Whore! A piece of Shit! Bag of Garbage! Useless trash! Baby killer!" one person after another screamed out. It seemed like the judge allowed them to behave that way on purpose and waited longer than she should have, to stop their disturbing behavior.

"Order in the courtroom," she finally said in a stern voice and banged her gavel against the sound block on her desk.

Natalia was still looking down, not disagreeing or denying anything they were saying. She believed that she deserved it and what happened in that alley was without a doubt, a genuinely criminal act. Who else would leave her child in the dumpster?

"Do you have any last statements you want to put on record Mr. Shlangovich?" the judge addressed the public defender.

"Yes, your honor," he answered. "I would like to address the court and add my statement to the record."

The young lawyer worked for the court and represented hopeless cases of people who couldn't afford experienced attorneys. Just like the prosecutor, he looked very young, and the only thing that was giving him a mature look was his black suit. During the trial, he didn't do much, other than cross-examine the witnesses that the prosecution provided. It would have been a waste of his time trying to get a not-guilty verdict for Natalia. She was a prostitute who conceived at 16, had a child at 17 and then to top it all off, she left her newborn in the dumpster to die, with no witnesses to prove otherwise. Of course, he still tried to show off his book smarts during the hearings, but as a first-year practicing attorney, it was only to gain experience in the courtroom.

"Your Honor, my client was only 17 years old when she delivered her child. She has been without parents since her 14th birthday, which is over four years as of this moment. Ms. Lebedeva turned 18 just two weeks ago, so she should be considered as a minor when the trial was taking place. We can all agree that she is young and immature, but we can also agree that her case is not as clear as the prosecution paints it to be. The defendant has said it herself. She was not thinking clearly and chose the wrong path in life; plus, there are important things to consider here! Ms. Lebedeva could have fled the city right after she allegedly left her child in the dumpster and no one would even know who she was or where to find her; but, she didn't. Instead, she jumped out of the moving vehicle and escaped from those who kept her in captivity. She testified under oath that she searched for hours to find the nearest police department to report what had happened. She told them everything: about the organization; her baby and about being forced to leave her child in the dumpster. She begged the police to help her find that alley; instead, she got arrested and charged with attempted murder. As I said a few times during the month-long trial, many things here just don't add up. I would kindly ask this court to repeat this trial and to investigate what Ms. Lebedeva has reported to us. I would also ask your honor to consider the defendant as a minor at the time of her arrest, and..."

"Objection," shouted the pissed-off prosecutor.

"Sustained," the judge answered immediately.

"Thank you, your honor. May I say something?"

"Go ahead, Mr. Chlenov," answered the judge, "And you, Mr. Shlangovich, watch what you say."

In a voice hungry for Natalia's conviction, the prosecutor continued. "The defense is trying to confuse this court without having any evidence about their claims. Ms. Lebedeva didn't come to the police department to get help. She came to protect herself in case someone saw her committing the crime. It's that simple. The defendant went so far as to make up a tale of how she was sold to a human trafficking organization at 14 years old and was forced to have sex with random men, day after day, until that same night that she delivered her child. On top of that, she claimed that some killer and a woman she called Madam Liz locked her and the child in the trunk, and brought them to some alley. Then, forced her to throw the newborn into the dumpster and if she refused, they were going to kill them both. In her statement to the police, she wrote that after leaving her baby in the dumpster, she was forced back into the trunk and they were going to transport her to a new location. Finally, the defendant told the police and this court that as soon as the car got off the highway, she, by some miracle, pushed the lock from the inside and opened the trunk. At that point, she jumped out of the trunk and started to run through the streets and neighborhood, looking for the nearest police department. All this is entirely misleading and a simple work of the creative imagination of Ms. Lebedeva. To me or any intelligent person, this case is a no-brainer. It is a disturbing story of a troubled girl, who obviously was of lax behavior and simply not ready to mother a child!"

"Your honor, if I may?" jumped in Mr. Shlangovich.

"Yes, you may," answered the Judge.

He was getting a bit ticked-off at the way the prosecution was twisting and changing the story around.

"If Ms. Lebedeva had made up all of that, then where are her records? Where is her family and where does she live? Why hasn't anyone looked for her since she got arrested and why is it that no one, including me, can find information about her in the public or federal records? We only know her first name, last name and birthday. Even that information came from the defendant herself. All I am asking of this court is to consider that the month-long trial is not enough to convict the defendant of attempted murder. I kindly request that this honorable court at least make the decision based on the fact that Ms. Lebedeva was a minor at the time the alleged crime took place. Thank you. The defense now rests."

It seemed like all that discussion took hours, but in reality, it was now only 2:30 p.m. Strangely enough, while each party was addressing the court, the judge wasn't taking any notes, not even one. The whole process from the beginning to the end looked unfair and illegal.

The moment the public attorney finished, the judge spoke. "Defendant, please stand for the sentencing!"

Natalia slowly got up but was still looking down at the floor.

The judge continued. "Under the federal law of the city of the Moscow Supreme Court, the defendant, Natalia Lebedeva, date of birth April 1st, 1973, is found guilty of the attempted murder of her two-day-old daughter, born May 1st, 1990. This court took into consideration that the defendant was a minor while the crime was committed. With that said, per the statute

105 of USSR Code of Criminal Law, the defendant is to serve nine years, 11 months, and 27 days or a total of 3650 days of imprisonment at the Siberian Female Maximum Security Prison. The sentence is figured beginning the day of the initial arrest, with the remaining days equaling to 3287. The release date is April 28th, 2000. The sentencing will take effect immediately, and the prisoner can be transported right after she gives her statement. Ms. Lebedeva, you now have an opportunity to address the court, using the maximum time of three minutes or five short sentences."

Most of the people who were present in the courtroom started to get loud and showed their dissatisfaction with the shorter length of her sentence. The strange thing was that not one of those people had any connection to this case at all. These were just bloodthirsty outsiders, who had nothing better to do than to waste their day in the courtroom, watching the destruction of someone's life. The final sentencing, in any case, was the only time strangers could come in, so all of the people there were clueless as to what this case was composed of or what evidence either party had. These people formed their judgments solely based on what they heard this afternoon.

Natalia, still in shock from the verdict, looked up at the judge with pain in her eyes and spoke up in a shaky voice. "I am very sorry for what I did, and I will never forgive myself for it, but please, just give me my daughter back. I will do whatever I can to make up for what I did. I just want to hold my little girl. I haven't seen her in almost a year, and I miss her very much." Natalia was emotional with tears running down her face. Despite her life, she still had a naïve and open mind, just as a young child, who was trying to convince a parent of something that was important to her.

The judge seemed to care less about anything that Natalia

had to say. Before the poor girl was able to finish what she was saying, the judge grabbed the folder off of her desk and got up.

"All rise," said the court bailiff in a loud voice.

Everyone in the courtroom got up, and a split second later the judge disappeared behind the door in the back of the courtroom. Natalia was left standing there in shock with a broken heart and dashed dreams. It was clear that the decision for this case wasn't going to change and the judge had no plans to conduct another trial.

What no one knew is that this judge was very well aware of what had happened to the poor girl. The judge and most of her colleagues knew everything about that organization and how enormously influential it was. She knew that everything Natalia said was accurate. Unfortunately for innocent girls like her, the organization's clientele included big-name politicians, high-ranking individuals, and even some judges. Natalia was just another victim of the corrupt system and the criminals who were running it. Dozens of corrupt crooks had their dirty hands in the pot of gold, enjoying the treasure created by the tears and blood of innocent girls.

She could consider herself to be very lucky. Someone could have killed her by now. The criminals must have figured that she was nothing and had no one in the world who cared about her. It was way too easy to silence her. A quick trial and a very long prison sentence were all they needed.

Natalia stood there in total disbelief. Deep down inside, her public defender was feeling wrong and was trying to give her some words of advice. Poor Natalia was in too much shock and still wasn't paying attention. The public defender got annoyed and started to talk loudly right in her face.

"Ms. Lebedeva! Hellooo! Please pay attention! I'm trying to help you, and we only have about a minute left together.

My advice to you is to forget everything that happened in your life up until today. Forget about your daughter and the hopes of finding her. Concentrate on serving your sentence and stay out of trouble. I know that nothing about your trial makes any sense to you, but I have learned over the past few months that there isn't that much you or I can do. It's all up to the judge. It would have been just as bad if we had picked a trial by jury. The outcome would have been the same. My best advice right now is still the same; behave as well as you can while in prison. Sometimes, people can get out of there earlier for good behavior. Find an inmate that's respected by others and stick with her."

She was still not responding. A minute later, the courtroom's sheriff finished filling out Natalia's paperwork and came up, grabbing her by the handcuffs.

They exited the courtroom and went down the same corridor she had walked through before. Then they took two flights of stairs and ended up in the garage where a white van was already waiting. It was a medium-size vehicle used for transporting criminals to and from the nearby temporary holding center. From there, the convicts were sorted out and driven to their assigned prisons.

The way people treated Natalia up until now was undeniably terrible and heartbreaking. All of that was like a bouquet of beautiful roses. What she was to go through in the maximum security prison, was a bouquet of hard, sharp thorns.

CHAPTER FOUR

lthough Natalia had been through a lot, she was not by any means prepared for prison. The transition into an unknown environment was horrifying to her. She was anxious and scared.

The bus ride from Moscow to the prison took almost three days. Most of the convicts slept the whole way there and only woke up to go to the bathroom when the bus made its stops. Natalia was able to sleep for a few hours each night and the rest of the time she observed the beautiful nature that Mother Russia had to offer.

When the bus finally arrived, all the girls including her were ordered to line up. Then the guards on the bus let everyone out, one person at a time. The moment they got off the bus the female guards greeted them, by smacking every girl on her head as they came out.

"Let's go! It's not a trip to the park. Let's move!"

Svetlana, what's the holdup? Why are these new arrivals

being so slow?" asked another guard somewhere in the distance.

"They are dumb, slow turtles; that's why!" answered the first guard and laughed out loud. All the while the handcuffed inmates struggled to get out of the bus. When the last girl got off, the guards lined everyone up and prepared them for a welcome speech.

Natalia ended up being in the middle of the line. On the right side of her stood a tall, middle-aged woman, who kept swearing at everything and everyone loudly enough for Natalia and the other inmates to hear. On the left side of Natalia stood a short, skinny girl with a boyish haircut and pronounced collarbones. She hadn't stopped crying since the moment Natalia saw her on the bus. No one knew why she was so emotional, but the truth was that she just got transferred from a juvenile facility. She turned 18 a few months back and because she almost killed her 12-year old roommate, seven more years got added to her sentence.

All three female guards lined up in front of the line and began to look everyone up and down. They were comparing each of the new arrivals to some things that had been written out on clipboards.

"Well, well, well! Hellllo ladies! Welcome to your new cozy home," the first guard said in a loud voice. It was the same woman who was smacking the girls as they walked off the bus. "My name is Svetlana Molchanova. I am the head prison guard, and you don't want to piss me off, so today is your lucky day! Why might you ask? The answer to that is because you are all alive, breathing and not one of you is here on death row!"

Most of the inmates had their heads down and were too scared to look up, although the annoying woman next to Natalia seemed not to care as much as the others. She was still mumbling and swearing; just loudly enough to be heard by the girls standing on each side of her.

"Ladies, from this moment on, all twenty of the prison guards, staff members, and the prison's warden, who is very strict, now own your body and soul," announced the guard who was to the left of Svetlana. "You are not allowed to do or say anything that will insult anyone here, including the other inmates! There are a set of rules that you will obey, and if you break them, the punishment will follow immediately. At that point, you will most likely be wishing that you were sentenced to death instead."

"On the other hand, if you all treat everyone around you with respect and kindness, you will be able to leave here in one piece and maybe even transfer to a medium security prison sooner than later," announced the guard to the right of Svetlana. "You are all here for different crimes; but as you might know, out of over fifty thousand women in our country currently behind bars, this prison contains the worst of all of them. We encourage you to work hard, do your best, and evolve into good human beings!"

"You will all be given an outline with do's and don'ts, and try to ..." Svetlana started to finalize the speech but stopped abruptly. "What is that sound?" She continued, making a puzzled face. "I keep hearing some mumbling, but I can't make out where it's coming from." Of course, it was coming from the inmate next to Natalia, who apparently wasn't interested in what the guards had to say.

"I don't know but I thought I heard sounds as well," added another guard.

Svetlana took a few steps towards the line and moved her head closer to the inmates as she walked by them. Other guards joined her as well. Natalia knew that the trouble was here. What she couldn't understand is why the woman next to her wouldn't stop, even now, when the guards were almost in front of her.

"What is your name?" Svetlana asked the inmate as she finally found who was making the sounds.

"My name is Lena Voronina," the woman answered.

And what is the reason you are mumbling things out loud during our speech? Are you just disrespectful or do you simply not give a shit?" Svetlana added.

"I wasn't mumbling, I was swearing," Lena answered. That was the stupidest thing anyone could say in this situation.

"You were what?" Svetlana tried to clarify the inmate's answer. "You were swearing?"

"Yes, I was," answered the inmate and looked at Svetlana as if she wasn't afraid of any consequences.

"Oh really? How nice of you. Who exactly, were you swearing at, may I ask?"

"I was swearing at everything and everyone."

"Ok. Well, that was not a nice answer, and since you obviously don't respect our speech, you will now get a very different welcome."

Svetlana headed towards the end of the line, walked around it, and seconds later ended up right behind the rude inmate. No one dared to move or look up, not even Natalia, who was an inch away from Lena Voronina.

The moment Svetlana came up close enough, she pulled out her rubber stick and struck the inmate right on the back of her knees. Because of her large size and the fact that her hands were in cuffs behind her, it was hard for Lena to control her balance. The fall was hard. She screamed out and dropped to the ground, hitting the asphalt, her knees first and then her forehead. Svetlana quickly took her rubber stick and placed it between the inmate's arms and back.

"Now try to get up! Go ahead and swear at the same time if you wish to," ordered the now-angry guard.

The woman struggled and somehow got back up on her knees. Then she slowly got to her feet. Because of the position of that rubber stick, she couldn't straighten all the way up and had to stand in a bent-over position. She looked very uncomfortable.

Natalia noticed a small amount of blood on the asphalt, and it reminded her of those drunken clients and the parties where she got beat up and abused. She wasn't planning on getting on the wrong side of any of the guards here. She was already scared.

Svetlana pushed the inmate out of the main line and forced her to walk towards the main gate. She whistled a short but creative melody to guards in the tower and a second later the electricity to the gate was deactivated. Svetlana unlocked the gate with her right hand and pushed the inmate through. That was the last time Natalia saw Lena Voronina for the rest of the day.

As soon as Lena and the guard disappeared into the building, the other two guards ordered the rest of the line to head toward the main entrance. The line was moving very slowly.

"Let's see. Let's see," said one of the guards who held a clipboard with the list of all of the inmates and their crimes by statute number. "It looks like we have no real killers in this batch. We might even take off your handcuffs."

Six guards were waiting for the new arrivals on the other side of the gate, and as soon as everyone walked through, the electricity went back on. The guards came up to the line and started to take the girls' handcuffs off. It looked a little chaotic for a moment, but when the cuffs were off, the line became orderly again.

"Ok, ladies, it's wash-up time. Take off your clothes and

line up against the wall so we can get you cleaned up and dressed," ordered one of the guards and pointed at the stone wall to the left of her. All the girls started to undress, and when they didn't move fast enough, some of the guards grew impatient. They came up to the slowest girls and began to take off their clothes for them.

Natalia surely knew how to undress quickly and easily. Within a few seconds, she was completely naked and walked right up to the wall to wait for the others. A few of the guards saw that and gave her a barely-noticeable smile. They were pleased with her speed and respectful manner.

When all the girls were ready, the guards ordered all the girls to turn around and face the wall. Another unpleasant memory flashed through Natalia's mind. Igor, the first in-house pimp she had, made her do the same thing and then hosed her down with a strong force of cold water beating down on her small body. At least she knew now what was coming and was mentally ready.

When she heard the sound of the water coming out of the hose, she spread her legs and arms against the wall. The guards now noticed that Natalia was not only obedient but also had a perfect body. Standing there naked she looked like a painting of "Venus" by Velazquez from the mid-1600s; not the usual look of a criminal or an inmate.

As soon as the water hit her body, her memories returned yet again. It was just as cold as it was before. The only difference was that Natalia's emotions and mind were completely under her control. Even though it seemed like her life was getting worse with every passing year, she concentrated on a brighter future, serving her sentence, and finding her daughter. It was clear; no one should underestimate the power of positive thinking and faith, even during the times when it seems that things cannot possibly get any worse.

The unwelcome shower lasted no more than five minutes, and at the end of it, Natalia was the only one standing. The hard water pressure forced the rest of the inmates to get down on the ground. Half of them were crying and trying to hide behind each other while the rest were curled up in a ball on the floor like helpless newborn children.

"Ok, ladies, let's line back up. It's time to go. We will be heading to the library where you will get your beautiful new black and white pajamas, as well as your inmate numbers. You will also be able to review and sign the rule books and get your starter allowance of 10 rubles," ordered the guards as soon as the hoses were shut off.

The scared inmates slowly got up off the floor and lined up again. Those who had been crying stopped sobbing, and those who were shaken up seemed to be getting back to normal. Natalia was the first in line, and the rest lined up behind her.

"Ok, ladies, no messing around. We are still letting you stay free of handcuffs for the next part of the admission, so please show us some appreciation," announced one of the guards.

All the guards in this prison were female. You would think that they were from the same family as they all looked like they could be sisters. It was almost as if they were all chosen on purpose to look like one another. They were all on the heavy side, taller than the average girl and dressed in the same type of uniform. Their short spiky hair covered by unusually shaped military hats, made them look even more alike; all but one. The head guard, Svetlana Molchanova, had long blond hair, mostly pinned together under her hat.

When all the girls got into the next room, Natalia was in a bit of a shock but this time in a positive way. The prison library was as beautiful as if it had been inside a mansion. There must have been a couple of thousand books there. The old carvings on the legs of the bookshelves made them look like something from the sixteen century.

"You like it, huh?" asked one of the guards.

Natalia just nodded her head up and down and continued walking. She didn't want to hold up the line, although she was still admiring the work of a very talented artisan.

"This is for the guards and the others who work here. We can come here and read during our lunch or dinner. Most of the inmates here forgot how to be human beings, so they aren't allowed in here."

It sounded alarming, but Natalia had zero knowledge of prison life and didn't read anything into it. Plus, as soon as all the girls were inside the library, one of the guards started the call-out, checking everyone's name on the list.

"Ok, ladies, you can now get your first set of pajamas with your inmate number and then walk over there and get the list of rules to read," said a different guard and pointed to the end of the library. Since Natalia was first, she walked over to the guard who was holding the prison pajamas and lifted them gently from her hands.

"Thank you very much," she said in a soft and quiet voice.

"Thank you?" answered the surprised guard. "Ok, you are welcome," she added and looked at the other guards who were also surprised. They hadn't gotten a thank-you from an inmate in many years. Natalia's personality was naturally earning the guards' sympathy without her even knowing it.

When she put on her new prison pants and shirt, she looked even more out of place. At least now, her perfect figure was covered up. Still, her beautiful long hair and flawless facial features were going to make her stand out from the crowd.

After everyone in line had gotten dressed, the guards

counted and cross-checked all the girls against the inmate number on their chest pockets. Natalia's inmate number was 78784867: nothing special about it at first glance but something was calling out to her. She was going to play with those numbers later on and see if anything was interesting about them. One of the guards grabbed a thick folder and gave a packet to each of the inmates.

"Ok, so here is the most important part of your check-in. You have fifteen minutes to read these few pages and sign your name on the last page. Understand?" the guards announced loudly and clearly.

"Yes," everyone answered in unison.

At the time Natalia was sentenced, Russia was still USSR, which consists of a union of fifteen Socialist Republics. The President, Mikhail Gorbachev, had not yet initiated the great fall of the Soviet Union that allowed many republics to become independent countries. The vast, worldwide economic downturn, especially USSR's economy, and the change of its name to the Russian Federation or Russia were going to happen in two more years. So far, everything was running great, and no one was yet affected.

The stable economy was the main reason every new inmate was given 10 rubles upon her arrival. That was a tenth of the minimum monthly wage but still enough to get the inmates through the first couple of weeks. They used it for extra food and snacks. The women were also able to purchase better soap and shampoo if they needed it.

Most of the newbies were put to work a day or two after their arrival. The first paycheck was two weeks later and in the form of a deposit into the inmate's account. The reason the initial gift got implemented is that most of the inmates had no family support. They were pretty much on their own.

For those who did have some family or friends to help them out, the help was quite minimal.

The issue was that there were no transfers or banks nearby, and cash had to be hand-delivered straight to the prison. With such an unfavorable location in the depth of Siberia, many of the family members couldn't take a week or more out of their lives just to bring some money. Heavy snowfalls during winter made that even worse.

"Ok, ladies, you can start now. Oh, and when you finish, bring the signed packet back and get your 10 rubles, provided to you by your honest government," she sarcastically added.

At least a third of those women were illiterate. They turned right to the last page and signed it. "Why aren't you reading it first?" Natalia whispered to the girl next to her.

"Why? Because I don't know how to read, that's why. I have been in different gangs on the streets since I was a teenager. That's why! Is that ok with you?" the girl replied. She was in her early 20's but already filled with hate and anger. Natalia felt terrible and was about to ask the girl if she wouldn't mind letting her read it, but one of the guards walked up to them.

"Why are you two talking? Just read and sign! It's that easy!" the guard said raising her eyebrows. "If you can't read it, then just sign it!" she added, loudly enough for everyone to hear. "If we read everything to all the convicts here, we would be spending a day a week doing so," the guard added a little softer, only addressing Natalia.

"Ten minutes left," announced another guard and Natalia realized that she had better get familiar with the packet before the time ran out and she would be left clueless about any of the prison's rules. She looked down and started to read.

Forgive Me, Nadia

Inmate Information Handout
Federal Bureau of Prisons
Maximum Security Female prison
Colony #6

The following are the rules implemented by the prison's director, Jana K. Vasilevna on September 5th, 1980 with the most updated revision published on January 1st, 1986.

1. The inmates are not allowed to abuse or harass the staff, the guards, the director or any other inmates: verbally, physically, or emotionally.
2. The inmates are not allowed to take any food from the cafeteria.
3. The inmates are not allowed to inappropriately expose their bodies either within their cells or outside of their cells.
4. The inmates are not allowed to have financial, romantic, sexual or friendly relationships with any of the prison's representatives.
5. The inmates are not allowed to have any sexual intercourse with other inmates with or without consent.
6. The inmates are not allowed to steal or take the belongings of any value from other inmates or the prison staff.
7. The inmates are not allowed to destroy or abuse the property of this prison, either inside or outside.
8. The inmates are not allowed to discuss their past crimes or to force other inmates to talk about theirs.
9. The inmates are responsible for folding their mattresses in half with the blanket wrapped on top, before 07:30 military time for the daily check of their cell.
10. The inmates are to have a monthly physical examination without any prior notice or consent.
11. Any new rules could be added or implemented without prior notice and at the discretion of the prison warden.
12. Any rules or regulations not followed by any inmate presently serving time in this prison, will result in immediate consequences and quarantined isolation. The length of the punishment is to be determined by the director.

Natalia finished reading the packet within a few minutes. After signing it and handing it over to the guard, she got her 10 rubles and placed them into her front pocket. At this point, Natalia didn't know how the money was going to get used, but those 10 rubles were going to get cherished, that's for sure. It was the first cash she had ever gotten from anyone.

As part of the procedure, one of the guards again handcuffed Natalia and the other inmates who had signed the booklet and had gotten their allowances. A moment later another guard came up to Natalia and told her that she was now going to bring her to the cell. Natalia was scared, and she hoped that it would be at least similar to what she had seen at the holding house while awaiting her trial. Unfortunately, the cell wasn't anything like what she had seen.

The moment she and the guard walked out of the library, lots of loud noises filled the air. The closer they came towards the central section, the louder it got. As they started to pass by the first cells, Natalia was looking from side to side, trying to see who was on the inside of those cells and if noises were coming from them. She couldn't see a thing.

The building had only one floor and a basement. All the regular cells that were single or double occupancy were on the main floor. They were lined up in a row across from each other, separated by a ten-foot wide hallway. For those who broke the rules, there were particular isolation and quarantine cells as well. They were all in the basement.

At least the first dozen cells on both sides of the hallway were the single occupancy ones. That's where all the worst of the worst from the whole country were. Those women were anything from serial killers and rapists to terrorists and even cannibals. They were all charged with multiple counts, and most of their sentences were death penalties by lethal injection.

Natalia couldn't see them because their cells had a thick metal door as well as bars on each side of it. There was only a small square window through which they got their food. On a regular day, the only time those inmates left the cell was to go for a one-hour-a-day walk in a small, specially designated area. They were not allowed to eat with the rest of the inmates or talk to anyone other than the guards. The cells were 6 feet by 4 feet, and the metal bed was only two by four. It wasn't even big enough for their whole body to fit on it comfortably. The pillow they used was three inches deep, and they had a thin blanket that was only big enough to cover half of their body. The toilet and the sink made of metal were attached to the bed.

No sounds were coming from those single cells. Most of the screaming, banging on the bars and singing of the national anthem was coming from the regular double-occupancy cells that Natalia and the guard were now passing by. If she didn't know better, she would think it was a psycho ward or an asylum.

"Don't pay attention. We have lots of mental cases here. They have no class and are worse than animals," said the guard. She must have sensed that Natalia was getting scared. After another minute of walking, it got quieter, and they finally arrived at Natalia's cell.

"Here it is: your new home for the next few years," said the guard. "It's much nicer in this end, and most of the girls here are newbies or the quiet type, just like you."

Natalia was anxious to see who the inmate that she will be living with was. The poor girl was hoping that it was someone friendly and kind. Again, she didn't get that fortunate.

"Ok, face the bars," ordered the guard. Natalia stopped and stood to face the cell. Her eyes were closed, as she was concentrating on staying calm. The guard opened the door and brought

Natalia in, took off the handcuffs and locked her up inside. It was after eight in the evening, and the cells only stayed unlocked between 6 p.m. and 8 p.m.

"Ok. Well, good luck to you and stay out of trouble, or we'll move you into the middle section where the crazies are," the guard said and walked away.

The poor girl didn't know what to do or what to expect. She turned towards the back of the room and started to check her surroundings. Suddenly the dirty room she had suffered in for most of her pregnancy seemed like a spacious apartment.

The double-occupancy cell she moved into was 6 feet wide and 9 feet long. It had a metal bunk bed attached to the right wall, a metal toilet, and a sink right across from it and a small, square window way up by the ceiling. Its multiple thick bars blocked almost half of the light coming in from the outside. The brick walls made the room feel cold, and the mattress was so thin that it looked more like a blanket.

She scanned the room, and her eyes locked onto her new roommate. The woman looked very masculine and, if not for her big breasts, she could easily be mistaken for a man. She didn't seem that threatening but then Natalia didn't know anything about her. Judging by the fact that the woman was sitting on the bottom bunk, Natalia figured that she would have to take the top one; not that she minded it anyway. It was closer to the window and the light.

"Whatever rules they made you read, I have my own in here!" said the roommate in a monotonous voice.

"Ok, I have no problem with it. Just let me know what the rules are," answered Natalia as she came up to the metal ladder to climb up to her bed.

"Well, rule number one is this," the woman said as she blocked the ladder with her arm. "If I'm not asleep and still sitting on my bed, you cannot go up to your bunk. I am not comfortable you doing that when I am awake, just in case you fall," she added.

Instead of questioning such an outrageous rule, Natalia moved away from the ladder and took a couple of steps towards the other wall. "Ok, no problem. I understand. I will wait until you fall asleep," she answered in a calm and collected manner.

Her roommate looked a bit confused and even surprised. That was undoubtedly not the answer she expected to hear. "Rule number two," she continued. "Don't talk to me unless I talk to you."

"Ok, no problem."

"Ok, no problem? Hmmm, ok then rule number three is just because we are in the same cell doesn't mean you can sit next to me in the cafeteria.

"Ok," Natalia kindly smiled.

"Really? Ok, then how about rule number four – don't make any sounds while I am sleeping. If you wake me up, I will smack you."

"Ok, I will stay quiet." Again, Natalia agreed.

It seemed like the inmate was trying her best to get under Natalia's skin but was not successful at it. After rule number four, she stopped, lay down and faced the wall.

Natalia, knowing that she could not go up to her bunk just yet, sat down on the cold floor. She was exhausted from the long ride, stressful welcome, and an awful environment. Plus, it was almost ten at night. Without realizing it, she slowly rested her head on top of her knees and drifted off to sleep. Even the bright lights that stayed on until midnight couldn't keep her awake.

The next morning she had to dive right into prison life. The schedule was very set and straight-forward. The wake-up siren went off at 6 a.m. The check-up on the prisoners and the general count was at 6:30 a.m. The cells got unlocked at 7 a.m., and everyone from the general inmate population reported to work at 8 a.m.

The workday was ten hours long with one thirty-minute break for lunch. All the inmates were back in their cells by 7 p.m. after which the doors were locked by 8 p.m. The siren to go to sleep went off at 10 p.m. If anyone disturbed others during the night, they would be removed and brought into the isolation area which was the last place anyone wanted to go.

Natalia was assigned to work in the textile wing, making shirts and dresses. She didn't know how to but learned her new skill within the first hour. Most of the skinny and smaller girls were kept inside and put to work in all different areas of the prison. The strongest and heaviest girls were put to work outside, especially during the winter months with high snowfalls. Shoveling the snow was the most challenging assignment to do, and the heftier inmates were the best candidates to do it.

Natalia preferred being inside anyway. It felt safer and more secure, at least for the first few days, until she got unwanted attention from some of the troubled inmates. Not only was Natalia a newbie but also the youngest and the prettiest one there. Those are the things that made her an unfortunate target for the hardship she was about to experience.

Even though the prison was maximum-security, the regular cell doors were still unlocked twice a day, before and after work. Those two-time slots were when the most troubles arose.

There were two main gangs in that prison. Both were under the control of two women who ironically were there for the same crime. They were both serving 25 years to life for killing their husbands. They were also the most influential and respected inmates there. For the newbies to get into the gang, they had to do a few required things. Most of those involved sexual favors, giving up all their earnings, and beating up one of the members of the other gang. Giving massages and cleaning cells and toilets were also part of the deal, at least for the first few months.

The only reason anyone would be interested in joining a gang would be for protection. Natalia had no desire for any of that; plus, those prison rules that she signed were in her head. She didn't want any issues. Unfortunately, they wanted her, and in an unexpected way.

Natalia was at the end of the line in the cafeteria, about to grab the metal tray with the preset dinner. The prison's staff didn't care if any of the inmates were vegetarians or had any allergies. You got what you got. Eat it or leave it. She took the tray and headed towards the empty table in the far corner. She had been eating alone since she got there but preferred it that way. To her, it felt safer and more comfortable.

When she had only a few steps to go, another inmate stuck her foot out, Natalia tripped over it and fell on the floor with her tray. The food went all over the place, and some of the apple juice splashed on the inmate who made her trip.

"What the fuck do you think you are doing, bitch?" screamed the inmate and got up from the table. She must have been at least a full head taller than Natalia. Her buzzed haircut made her look like a mean guy who was looking for trouble.

The poor girl knew that arguing or explaining herself was pointless and the woman was apparently trying to start a fight. "I am sorry," said Natalia and grabbed the bottom of her shirt, using it to wipe the juice off of the inmate.

"Get your fucking hands off me! What the hell is wrong

with you?" she screamed in Natalia's face. "If you are in a cleaning mood then just get down on your knees and clean between my legs," the inmate added and started to laugh out loud. The rest of the people at her table and other inmates who heard them were shouting as well. The guards didn't see how Natalia fell and they weren't going to get involved anyway. It seemed like they picked and chose their battles.

Natalia didn't say anything back to the other inmate and just got down on the floor to clean up what she could. After she finished, she walked over to her table and sat down, placing the now empty tray in front of her. It was sad and unfair, especially since prisoners were not allowed to get another tray of food.

For Natalia, the dinner couldn't come to an end fast enough. She tried to keep her eyes down, but every time she looked up, other inmates smirked at her, showed their tongues and blew her kisses. All that was making Natalia more and more uncomfortable and her anxiety grew with every passing minute.

When dinner was finally over, and everyone lined up for the count, one of the inmates behind Natalia whispered in her ear. "That's why you're better off getting into a gang. At least you no one will pick on you. As long as you don't mind doing sexual favors and a few other things, you will be much better off." Natalia knew that the girl was right, and that was the only way to stay safe, but she just couldn't do it.

When she finally got back to her cell, the door was still open. Natalia's roommate hadn't arrived yet, so she decided to get up to her bunk quickly. She was tired and upset about what had just happened.

A few minutes later, five solidly built women showed up at the cell. Their smiles confused Natalia a bit, but she didn't show it. The woman in the front who was the biggest of them all kept strangely licking her lips. Natalia had no idea what the visit was all about. She recognized one of the inmates since she was the one who made her trip but Natalia knew that all of these women were undoubtedly familiar with the prison's rules and weren't going to hurt her. She was wrong.

"Ladies, I will go first. Watch the door and block the wall," the woman said out loud, addressing her friends.

"Hello, there pretty girl!" She looked at Natalia, smiled, and took a big step forward. "My name is Marsha, but everyone calls me Godmother! You have to call me Mama because from now on you are going to be one of my babies!"

Natalia was confused, but her gut feeling was telling her that this Marsha – or Godmother - was up to no good. "I didn't do anything wrong. I fell by mistake," she answered, thinking that their visit had something to do with what happened earlier.

"Oh, I know you didn't do nothing wrong sweetheart! The one who created you also didn't do anything wrong," laughed the Godmother and took another step forward.

"What do you want?" Natalia asked softly.

"I want you. We all want you. Why else would we come here? Plus, if you are good to us, I'll make sure that there will always be just us, me and these ladies here."

"I don't get it. What exactly do you want me to do?"

"I will show you what I want you to do! It's easier just to do it than to explain it. Don't worry; I will be gentle for the first time," said Marsha and grabbed Natalia by her ankles.

"What are you doing? Don't touch me," screamed Natalia and tried to get her foot out of Godmother's manly hands. Marsha was way too forceful and too experienced in these types of scenes. Natalia was merely no match for her or any of them.

She pulled Natalia off the top bunk, dropped her onto the bottom bed and sat down on the girl's legs. Then she covered Natalia's mouth with one hand and began to undress her with the other. Marsha was forceful and very strong.

For the next 15 minutes, Natalia re-lived many of the disturbing scenes from her past. There were the nights when she was abused and tortured by drunken men at the parties and the days when groups of clients tied her up and took their turns on using her. The Godmother's arms and body felt just like those men.

The other inmates who came with the Godmother were blocking the whole cell. They were ensuring that no one could see what was happening inside and at the same time watch out for the guards.

A couple of minutes into the struggle, Natalia's clothes were on the floor next to the bed. A few more minutes after that, Godmother finished and got up off of Natalia's face. She then quickly pulled up her pants and took a deep breath.

"Wow! That was amazing!" she said, looking at the quietly crying Natalia. The Godmother turned towards the other inmates and smiled "Ladies, this girl is sexy and good as hell!"

"Oh, we can't wait to get a piece of that," replied one of the other inmates. Her eyes were burning with desire.

"Yeah, that's right! I want to go next," added another one and took a few steps towards the bed.

"Of course, go right ahead. I already warmed those hot lips up for you. Hahaha," replied Marsha and walked towards the others to help cover the door.

For the next few weeks, Natalia was raped almost daily by the Godmother and the other inmates. On some occasions, when she would put up a fight or couldn't take so many rapes in a row, they would beat her up. Usually, they would hit her legs, arms, and butt; anywhere but the face, so the bruising wouldn't attract the attention of the guards. The Godmother loved Natalia's beautiful face, blond hair, and perfect body. Natalia, being the most beautiful there, became the unluckiest one. The situation was alarming.

Along with the physical abuse and rape, Natalia was made to do all the dirty work that the other gang members didn't want to do. She cleaned urine and feces-covered toilets. She scrubbed the floors in their cells with her shirt. On top of that, she was forced to give full body massages to Marsha and a few other members of the gang.

Natalia struggled with the abuse both physically and emotionally. She was only able to deal with it because she had already lived through many years of abuse. Strangely, her terrible past helped her build incredible inner strength and endurance. Her firm belief in better days was wholly unbelievable and almost hard to conceive.

About five weeks later the guards started to notice changes in Natalia's behavior. She wasn't finishing her food, her work wasn't high in quality, and she moved around at a much slower pace. Even her usual friendliness towards the other workers and the staff wasn't there anymore. The guards started to get more and more curious; but, it was the head guard Svetlana Molchanova, who decided to look deeper into her unusual behavior.

The next time that all the regular inmates were scheduled to shower, Svetlana switched with another guard on duty. She walked right over to Natalia the minute the girl finished her shower. As soon as Natalia saw Svetlana approaching, she grabbed a towel and covered her body up as fast as she could. It was too late. Svetlana saw dozens of bruises on Natalia's body, and she became livid.

Most of the time, the guards didn't get involved in the

fights between the inmates, mainly if it wasn't anything too dangerous; but at least they all knew about it. Now, it was a different story. Svetlana had no idea that Natalia had gotten abused, never mind to this extent.

"Natalia!" said Svetlana with an anxious tone. "We need to talk!"

Natalia didn't reply. She just looked at Svetlana in silence. Natalia knew that Svetlana noticed her bruises. She also knew that the punishment for her abusers was going to be very severe. There would be isolation and quarantine for many days in the basement, followed by possibly a longer prison sentence.

The inmates who already experienced the isolation cells were more afraid of going back to them then extending the time they had to serve. Those cells were terrifying to everyone. There was just darkness, 23 hours a day, with one hour outside. Those 23 hours, the inmate was locked up in there, completely alone. The cell was 6 feet by 6 feet but had no window or bed in it. The only things inside were a metal toilet and the sink. To sleep, the prisoner had to sit on the floor or crawled up into a ball.

As Svetlana and Natalia headed out of the shower room, the Godmother and her gang all watched. The poor girl wasn't looking up, but Svetlana did. She noticed Marsha and the others watching them with a nervous look in their eyes. Even though they were bullies, they were afraid of the guards and the consequences they could face.

About half an hour later, both Svetlana and Natalia came out of the guard's office. Together, they walked to Natalia's cell, and the guard helped her to get up to the top bunk. Svetlana covered her up with an extra blanket that she had brought with her and looked into Natalia's eyes one last time before leaving the cell.

"Are you sure you don't want me to arrange a different cell or maybe you would prefer to sleep on the bottom?"

"No, no, no, I don't want the bottom bunk, I don't!" answered the worried Natalia. "I spent enough time on it during the past few weeks, but thank you. You are very kind."

That was the most Natalia had said to the guard in the past half hour. It was clear to Svetlana that Natalia's abuse was sex-related and had taken place in that same cell. She felt terrible that it was done right under all the guards' noses and no one noticed a thing. In unexplained ways, Svetlana had developed a motherly love towards the humble Natalia, who touched her heart.

As soon as she exited the cell, another guard came up to her out of nowhere. "What's going on? Were you able to find out what happened and who abused her?" she asked.

"Nope, she wouldn't tell me anything, no matter what I said. When I asked for the names, she just shook her head, and when I started to guess who the abusers were, she didn't even acknowledge me," answered Svetlana. "Wait a minute," she paused and said, "How do you know what topic I was discussing with Natalia? I didn't tell anyone. How would you know about the abuse?" she added suspiciously.

The other guard realized that she was getting herself into deep trouble and came up with a quick but feeble reply. "Well, you know how these convicts are! They have big mouths and talk too much. It's just a rumor," she answered back, looking away.

"Is that right? Ok, and do those rumors mention who put this poor girl through hell and why her body and her inner thighs are black and blue?" Svetlana asked in a raised voice. She was not stupid and hated it when her intelligence was insulted by inmates or even by the other guards. She knew there was much more to the story and she was going to get to the bottom of it.

"No, I haven't heard anything else," snapped the other guard and walked away.

Natalia didn't know it yet but that day was a significant turning point in her life. The strength she was born with was now blooming like a wildflower. Her kindness and humble ways helped her to live through another dark part of her already tough life. She stayed true to herself. Through yet another hardship and pain, she had earned her title of being "unbroken."

CHAPTER FIVE

The very next day things started to change, and the difference was pretty noticeable. For the first time in a few weeks, the Godmother and her gang didn't show up at Natalia's cell. None of them ever came up to her cell again. They didn't bother her in the yard, at the cafeteria or even in the shower. They were acting like they didn't even know her.

Natalia was a bit surprised and yet grateful that they finally left her alone. She had no idea what happened and why they backed away. The truth was that her silence earned respect from them and that was what she so deeply deserved. The Godmother and others knew very well that Natalia had kept her mouth shut when Svetlana questioned her. They understood that Natalia saved them from all the pain and suffering they rightfully deserved. Sometimes, respect for others is earned not by creating fear, but by forgiving them their sins.

Natalia never brought up what she experienced, and no one questioned her about it. She just moved on and continued dreaming about her positive future, surviving through her lengthy prison sentence and finding her daughter. She also prayed for all the guards and asked God to give them the patience, kindness, and understanding they needed to be able to watch over the inmates peacefully.

On the last Sunday of every month, the priest visited that prison. The wake-up siren would go off at 5:15 in the morning instead of 6:00, giving the inmates time to wake up and prepare for his arrival. Usually, he showed up around 5:30 and left before 6:00. That's when the doors of the majority of the cells were unlocked. He would walk the floor from cell to cell and bless all the inmates with holy water.

The last time he came there Natalia was on her bed, holding her stomach in pain from the physical and sexual abuse. She wasn't able to get up and stand by the bars to get a few drops of holy water. This time Natalia was up and ready at 5:30 while her roommate was still asleep. She was standing right by the door, patiently waiting for the priest.

When the priest finally made his way to her cell, he blessed Natalia with the holy water, but to her surprise, he didn't leave right away. He paused and looked directly at her. Then, as if he felt the need to, he started to read a prayer to her and made a cross in front of her face.

"Father, I know that you know my future. God must have told you whether I make it or not! Please give me some guidance!"

The priest smiled at her and said, "My child, you are an angel! You are destined for greatness! Our Dear Father is watching you every moment. You have saved your soul and the souls of others from pain and suffering. Many already are questioning why they have forgotten their God! You are the one who made them ask for forgiveness. Continue helping them see the light, and you will always be blessed! You ARE a survivor, Natalia!"

"Thank you, Father! I will. I really will," she answered with her hands clasped in prayer. "I don't know how I have helped someone already, but I will do my best," she added.

Only after the priest walked away did she realize that she had never told him her name, nor was it displayed anywhere on her clothes or the outside of her cell. She had no idea how he knew it, but she distinctly heard him say "Natalia." She also had no idea whom she had helped and how or what she needed to do to move forward. One thing she did know was that her time in prison was there for a reason and that was to help others.

For the next few days, Natalia stayed quiet but happy. She was trying to brainstorm and find the answer within her heart as to what was her destiny. She was trying to get to the bottom of when and how she could help others. The answer suddenly came to her.

Without planning or thinking much about it, Natalia started to talk to other newbies: those who arrived with her and those who got there after she did. Most of them were doing well on their own, but a few had joined the gangs.

The tall woman, who got in trouble when her group first got off the bus, wasn't around much. She worked outside and stayed to herself in the yard and the cafeteria. Some of the inmates said that she was crazy and that the three days she spent in quarantine pushed her to the edge.

When it came to the skinny girl who cried non-stop and couldn't read, she seemed to adjust very well. It appeared that no one picked on her. Maybe it was because they knew she had been behind bars for many years in a juvenile detention facility. A prison is a prison no matter what level it is. She became friends with a few of the other skinny girls since they all worked together in the kitchen. It was a bit funny how the smallest of the inmates got assigned to the kitchen. It must have been because the guards knew that those girls wouldn't eat that much while they were cooking for the rest of them.

Overall, things were going very well. Somehow, in magically smooth ways, Natalia's life there became more comfortable and less stressful. She was transforming into a more outspoken girl who had no problems helping other inmates with little things that were important to them. Natalia showed them everything from how to fold their blankets quickly, to what prayer is and how to pray to the Universe and God. She also spread the message among the inmates about the hardships the guards had to endure while working there. Natalia told the girls that the guard's jobs were tough and stressful, which was why most of the guards and staff acted cold and distant.

One early morning as Natalia was lying on her bed visualizing and dreaming about brighter days, a fantastic idea came to her. It was something that she had already thought of, but she was too busy working and too shy to speak out.

The time in the library when the skinny girl couldn't read the rules of the prison hadn't left Natalia's mind. She wanted to do something about it, so she decided to help that girl and other inmates. Natalia liked the idea of teaching them how to use basic grammar, how to read and do simple math. The very next morning she designed a plan and put it into action.

She started by teaching girls how to say different phrases accurately and how to speak in a clear and understandable manner. Then she showed them different grammatical rules by drawing them in the air. It was an unusual way to teach, but it worked. Natalia did that every single day during lunch and dinner.

Interestingly enough, more and more inmates joined her during those lessons. Every table near her was full of girls from all different backgrounds. If they couldn't sit down somewhere near her, they would listen and eat while standing up. They just wanted to be able to hear the stories, teachings and exciting facts that she so loved to share.

When she noticed way too many inmates gathering around her instead of using their lunch break to eat, she decided to add more time to teach. She utilized the time everyone had on the outside. There, she was able to explain simple math problems using different leaves, grass and other things she could find. Even during the cold months, her creativity didn't cease to amaze. When the beautiful white snow covered the prison's yard, she still held her classes and drew the math problems in the snow using her fingers. It was a very amusing site. Natalia looked like a teacher who was writing on the classroom blackboard with chalk.

Remarkably, with time even gang members started to show up to her lessons. Also, the Godmother, who never showed any curiosity or interest in education, came around and tried to listen in. It was evident that Natalia was creating total magic with her bare hands and pure heart. She was transforming hundreds of criminals into educated and possibly better citizens of society. She was teaching them valuable yet straightforward things that no one, not even their parents, had taught them.

Amazingly enough within a few months, the disturbance rate among the inmates went down substantially. There were almost no fights, and those that happened were all verbal. The gangs were not bullying others or the newbies who were arriving every couple of weeks. Most of the inmates who never wanted to be in the same room with each other were now laughing and having fun with best friends. If people could look at all the girls there without noticing their prison pajamas, they would think that they were at a cookout, spending quality time with those they loved.

Natalia became a savior for most and a tremendous asset to the correctional officers, who now were able to have free time and get back to reading at the library. As time went on, they allowed Natalia to take out books for herself and for teaching the lessons to others. Natalia was now highly respected and loved. It gave her a feeling of safety and contentment; although, she never stopped thinking about her past and the things she did wrong. She was still in fear that one day it would all come to the surface.

There was no doubt that she was grateful that the prison's privacy law was working very well and no one there knew what crime she had committed that had led to her imprisonment. Knowledge of that was not allowed, especially in the maximum security facility. Most of the guards didn't know either because all they knew was the number of the inmates' statute. That way they could not guess what the actual crime was.

No matter what crime the girls were there for, one thing they all frowned on the most was a crime that had anything to do with child abuse. In any given prison, those types of convictions were something that the general inmate population didn't take lightly. Sure they were all under one title that united them as criminals, but most of them were still sisters, mothers, and grandmothers.

Natalia knew all that from many conversations she had among the prison's population. She knew that the reaction of any given inmate to someone who abused or endangered a child was unpredictable. It's not like anyone there knew that

Natalia was a different person from a year or two ago. Natalia regretted her past life, and now she was changing and evolving. The rest was better off left unsaid.

The time started to fly by, and at the end of serving her second year, Natalia was suddenly requested to come into the office of the prison's warden. The fact that she was nervous was an understatement. The girl had never met the director or even spoke to any inmates who did. The only thing she knew was that the director was a woman, just like everyone who worked there and that she had strict values, higher than anyone else's. The head guard, Svetlana Molchanova, was the one whom the director sent to get Natalia.

"Mrs. Molchanova, do you know why the director is calling me?" asked Natalia in a worried manner, as they walked towards the office. Svetlana was keeping a steady pace while unlocking and locking dozens of metal-barred doors along the way. Natalia had never been in this part of the prison before. It was neat, clean and furnished well, giving it the look of a cozy apartment.

"Don't worry. You are going to be ok," answered Svetlana with a smile and continued walking. A minute later they were outside of the director's door. Svetlana knocked.

"Come right in," answered the warden.

"Address her by her first and last name. It's Jana Vasilevna," Svetlana whispered in Natalia's ear as she pushed the door open.

"Good Morning, Jana Vasilevna!" said the guard to the director and pulled Natalia by her sleeve.

"Good morning, Jana Vasilevna," Natalia repeated after her.

"Good Morning ladies, please come in," answered the director.

Natalia was astonished. Jana Vasilevna didn't look like a typical warden. Natalia expected to see someone like one of the guards or maybe even an inmate. It just made no sense.

She was unbelievably beautiful and elegant. Her facial features looked like a perfect mathematical calculation from the creator himself. Her long thin fingers with perfectly manicured nails and classy, bright red polish made her look very feminine. Her hands were gently crossed and placed on top of a burgundy leather notebook on her desk. Her reading glasses were resting precisely on the tip of her small nose making her look severe and stern. Her eyes were blue just like the clear, blue sky and black mascara complemented the shape of her eyes, making them stand out even more. Her blond hair was up, but you could tell it was long and wavy. She was wearing a nicely tailored gray suit and white low-cut button-down shirt, with cuffs sticking out from under the jacket sleeves. She looked modern and stylish.

"So, Ms. Lebedeva, it is a pleasure to meet you finally, and to put a face with the name," she addressed Natalia, who looked like she had frozen in her spot. The girl hadn't gotten past the point of trying to figure out how this beautiful woman could be a prison warden. "Ms. Lebedeva, are you ok?" asked the director, with a barely noticeable smile.

"Natalia, what is wrong with you?" whispered Svetlana. "Answer her immediately," she said and pulled Natalia by the hand.

Natalia snapped out of her mesmerized state and quickly replied, "It is also very nice to meet you, Jana Vasilevna."

"Please, have a seat. I just wanted to chat with you for a few minutes," the director kindly addressed Natalia.

Still keeping her eyes on the director, Natalia took a few steps forward and came up in between the two matching chairs that were in front of the desk. The chairs looked like someone had taken them out of a king's mansion. A master artisan must have carefully handcrafted the mahogany wooden back and armrests. The beautiful burgundy material made them look priceless.

"It's ok, Jana Vasilevna, I will stand. I sit a lot during the day anyway," said Natalia with wide-open eyes.

"Ok, suit yourself. I will also stand then. I sit all day as well. Trust me, my job has been quite boring, thanks to you," said the director and pushed her chair to the side.

The moment the warden got up, Natalia felt very humbled and flattered. The director of the maximum security prison was standing in front of her out of respect. That, mixed with a strange comment she just heard, was making Natalia feel almost uncomfortable. Not to mention, here she was, getting the best treatment from a woman she had met only a few minutes ago.

"So, Natalia, I have heard a lot of good things about you from the guards and others. Not only that, but I have seen a continuous improvement within this prison and among other inmates. I've been here for over fifteen years, and I have never had such a low in-prison crime rate and such a high compliance rate all at the same time. It was shocking that the overall production from our location is by far the highest it has ever been," the director said seriously. "Even my bosses have noticed the good results we have here for the first time in over a decade."

Natalia was trying to take in all that she was hearing, but none of it sounded real. It was like a dream that nobody wished to end. Everything just seemed too good to be true.

"In addition to that, a couple of days ago I received a personal, over-the-phone recognition by General Babnik, who is the head of all the prisons in the Soviet Union. After that, I received a written recognition and a raise in my salary, which I have not gotten in over eight years. I contribute this to you and only you. I honestly have never met anyone like you before. You are truly special and unique, and I know that you will go far."

Every word the director said sounded unreal. Natalia's face was displaying zero emotions. Svetlana was still behind her near the door, trying her best to control the tears that were forming in her eyes. The director's speech was making Svetlana very emotional. Natalia, on the other hand, had no tears. She had lost most of them the night she left Nadia in the dumpster, and the rest went away during the first month in that prison. She looked cold and insensitive.

"Natalia, I know you are shocked, and that's why I said that you are special. It is your humble and kind ways that have dramatically transformed this prison and the way we have to run it from now on. You opened up our eyes and hearts and made us see that even cold-hearted criminals are still human beings. We now believe that many of them are capable of change! For that, I thank you from the bottom of my heart. I started to enjoy coming to work, just like I did in the beginning. I know that all the guards and workers can say the same thing," she added. Something made Natalia snap out of her daze, and she realized that she had not yet thanked the warden for all her kindness.

"Thank you, Jana Vasilevna, I am very touched and humbled by your kindness. I try my best every day, and I don't expect anything in return!"

"I see that, and that's what makes you, you. So with all that said, I would like to reward your selfless acts of kindness with a little something that you might like." She paused and picked up the nicely crafted notebook from her desk.

"I heard that you love to read and in fact, you have read hundreds of books from our library! Is that true?"

"Yes, Jana Vasilevna, it is true. I read 355 of them, but some were short and quick. I love reading, and I love sciences, but I especially like numbers," Natalia answered in a much more comfortable manner.

"Hmmm. Very interesting. Well, I happen to love numbers as well, and even though I'm not super smart, I love the math and the science of numerology. Have you heard of that before?"

"Yes, Jana Vasilevna, I have. Believe it or not, you just reminded me that I haven't even checked my inmate number yet. I have been so busy that I forgot to do that since the day I got here. I believe that all the numbers in the universe stand for something and my inmate number is not an exception."

"You have been busy? Is that what you just said?" the director laughed out loud. "You are too funny! Yes, you were too busy, too busy helping hundreds of inmates to learn how to read, do the math and run a business! Right?" she added in a very caring voice. "I must say that you are the most remarkable twenty-year-old I have ever met!"

"Thank you. Thank you again, Jana Vasilevna!"

"Oh, my goodness, please stop calling me that already. It's way too formal! Just call me Mrs. Vasilevna. That's more than enough!"

"Ok, Mrs. Vasilevna, I understand." Natalia smiled.

"Ok, let's get to the main reason I invited you here. How would you like to earn your high school diploma?"

Natalia's eyes opened wide, "Excuse me? Can you please repeat that, Mrs. Vasilevna?"

"Sure, I was just asking if you would like to earn your high school diploma since you mentioned you were only able to finish the eighth grade."

"Uh yes, Mrs. Vasilevna, that would be a dream come true! Education is my biggest passion. The more education I have, the higher chance I have to find a better job when I get out of here. With a better job, I'll get more money, and that will give me an opportunity to find my . . ." Natalia caught herself.

"To find your daughter, is that what you were going to say?"

"Yes Mrs. Vasilevna, to find my beautiful daughter," answered Natalia as she looked at the floor. Her facial expression changed, and she became sad almost instantly.

"You know Natalia, I was also young and stupid, and did things that I still regret, but that's life, and you learn from your mistakes. People are not going to judge you if they don't know the details about your past. Just try to keep things to yourself. There is no need to give anyone ammunition that they could use against you. You are now older and more mature, therefore, do what your heart tells you and follow your gut feelings," said the director with genuine care in her voice. It sounded like loving advice from a mother to a daughter, and Natalia felt good hearing it at that very moment.

"Thank you very much, Mrs. Vasilevna. I appreciate your care and words of comfort. It means a lot to me," replied Natalia maturely and responsibly.

"Ok, so you said that you would like to earn your high school diploma and guess what? I have it here for you. You have already earned it!" She opened the notebook and took out a red leather diploma. "Here is the proof of your high school graduation, issued to you by Moscow High School #85, with a concentration in business and mathematics. The board of directors and upper-level educators approved all the materials that you needed for the completion and your graduation. Everyone agreed that between your reading, practicing, and teaching for the past two years, you have met all the requirements you needed."

The director walked around her desk and approached Natalia, who was now in even more shock. "You look like you are going to faint," she said to Natalia and hugged her gently and lovingly. "Here is the diploma! Take it!" She pulled away and handed the diploma to Natalia.

The girl was so stunned that she didn't even take the diploma out of the director's hands right away. All she could think about was that morning when the priest told her she is watched, protected and destined for greatness. He was right, and she now felt the genuine love and blessing of the universe.

The great deed the warden had just done undoubtedly changed Natalia's life for the better but giving her the diploma wasn't the only thing Mrs. Vasilevna had for her. Natalia was about to get an even more significant shock.

"Sweetheart, there is something else I have for you," smiled the director and locked her eyes on the still shocked Natalia. "I am authorizing your transfer as of tomorrow afternoon to a medium security prison. There you will be able to attend classes with real teachers and professors so you can earn your bachelor's degree in whatever profession your desire! Also, I made tomorrow a half-day for everyone so that you can say your final goodbyes. The bus will be leaving at 3 p.m., and you will be the only passenger on it, so don't be late," she said and playfully winked.

The shock of everything that was happening to her within the past half hour was making Natalia lightheaded. It was more than a dream. Against all the odds it was now a reality, and she finally got a chance for a better life.

"I don't even know what to say right now, Mrs. Vasilevna. I don't even know how to thank you for what you are doing for me," said Natalia. Her voice sounded shaky.

"You have done way more for me than I did for you, trust me on that! Now get out of here before I get too emotional. It took a lot for me to let you go, but you don't belong here any longer! Go and make me proud!" She walked behind her desk and faced the window, trying to hide her emotions and tears from Natalia and Svetlana.

"I will not let you down, Mrs. Vasilevna! I will never, ever let you down! I promise you I will remember this forever and ever," Natalia said with overflowing emotions! Her voice was loud and happy. She felt sad about leaving her students but was so grateful for the opportunity she got. Despite the horrendous abuse when she first got there, that prison became her first ever home and Jana Vasilevna became like her real mother.

Svetlana was still crying as if she were watching a soap opera on TV. It was apparent that as a correctional officer, she didn't get to see these kinds of magical moments too often. It was also evident that the director trusted Svetlana quite a bit. If she didn't, she would never have mentioned personal pieces of information from Natalia's life. Natalia turned around and headed to the door, holding on to her diploma for dear life.

"Natalia, wait. Look at the white piece of paper right there," said the director without turning around. She pointed to her desk. Natalia came up to the table and noticed a small piece of paper with some numbers and letters written on it.

Jana Vasilevna was still looking through the window but continued talking. "Last night I was able to figure out what your inmate number meant. I used the letters of the alphabet and matched them up with the numbers. Look at the result, please."

Natalia picked up the paper and read it. Her eyes opened wide in astonishment, and the note slipped out of her hand. The letters written under the numbers were:

Forgive Me, Nadia

7 8 7 8 4 8 6 7
S U R V I V O R

CHAPTER SIX

A ray of light was finally shining upon Natalia's life. The medium-security prison was much more pleasant than the other jail. The guards were younger and gave prisoners more freedom to do what they wanted.

The medium-security prison was much more pleasant than the other jail. The guards were younger and gave prisoners more freedom to do what they wanted. Most of the cells were open during the day and locked as late as 10 o'clock at night. The majority of the inmates behaved better than at the maximum security prison, and their sentences were noticeably shorter.

Although Natalia was looking forward to continuing her education, her second favorite part of the transfer was a new schedule. The work week was Monday through Friday and only 8 a.m. to 4 p.m. The new position was a teacher's assistant, and she loved it. In the evening she attended required classes for the completion of her first degree and the weekends she dedicated to her homework and reading. Out of almost three thousand women, she was the only inmate working toward an actual degree. She was fortunate, and she knew it.

Natalia made tons of friends from the very first day there. Some of them already knew of her through friends and the guards in both prisons. Some got to know her in the classrooms where she assisted different teachers with all kinds of tasks. Some were getting a stronger bond with her and were becoming close friends. Just like in the last prison, she got along with everyone, from inmates and guards to all the other workers.

The setup of this facility was different from the last one. The cells were built to house four to six inmates, and that made it more exciting and fun. Due to the overflow of convicts, the facility was way over its legal capacity. Each cell ended up housing up to ten people. The newbies were only able to use the beds when the other inmates were out and about. The new arrivals always had fewer comforts.

There were a few double-occupancy cells at the end, closer to the offices. These were specifically for women who were not emotionally stable or who had minor health issues. Initially when the prison got built, many decades ago, those cells were used for privileged inmates. Those included: actresses; singers; daughters of politicians and family members of someone in the service or police force. It was an era where money talked louder than the crimes. Those times have changed, and now it's even more unfair. Nowadays it's almost impossible to see someone from any of those categories serving their sentence here or anywhere else for that matter.

Natalia got assigned to one of the two single-occupancy cells available at that prison. Her cell had a more comfortable bed, a mini fridge, and even a coffee maker. Natalia got this cell because she was now a teacher's assistant and also needed a place to study. Her homework was just as complicated as it was for any other student at a typical college. Doing well in her classes required a more peaceful environment. Regardless, she truly appreciated her new home and treated the opportunity with great respect. Natalia's dreams and visions were slowly approaching, and it felt more real now than ever before. Now, the ocean of knowledge was entirely hers.

It took her a little under three years to finish her first bachelor's degree in business management. Then, it took her only one more year to get an additional degree in accounting. That made her very desirable to potential employers when she was finished serving her sentence.

What Natalia was able to accomplish inside of the prison walls and work at the same time was hard for many to comprehend. Every single teacher and professor was blown away by her discipline and dedication. Her many abilities and highest possible grades were mind-blowing and yet, just like before, Natalia stayed humble and grounded.

Their amazement of her didn't stop there. She used the little free time she had left on weekends and helped other inmates with homework and reading. Even on weekday nights, she would hold an hour writing class for the beginners after she finished her homework. As time went on, Natalia had earned their respect and her new title. Most of the inmates started to call her Ms. Lebedeva, not just Natalia.

Meanwhile, Natalia's perfect behavior and a complete dedication to everything she did made her yet again stand right out in the crowd. She was unique not only in the eyes of the guards but also in the eyes of the other inmates. Natalia became the one to whom everyone came for advice or to vent. She didn't mind it, and always found the time for them, even when she was exhausted. Serving others in any way Natalia could, added much more happiness and a pleasure to her life. She felt needed and useful.

Of course, a prison is still a prison, even if it's a medium security one with much more freedom. There were troubles and disagreements between different inmates or between inmates and the guards. Having a flexible schedule for everyone and a lot of free time before and after work, brought about its own set of issues.

The freedom that the inmates had at this prison helped to create a lot more intimate relationships. Unlike the maximum security facility where inmates got almost no time together, here the girls could spend hours with each other. On top of that, to complicate things a bit more, this facility was very close to the city and relatives or friends were able to visit the inmates much more often. That created an uneven financial level among the girls.

Here there were lots of couples with a considerable age difference between them. The older women usually had more available finances to provide a comfortable life for their younger partners. Of course, there was also an issue of paid sex, where those who had extra cash to spare would pay younger ones for 10-30 minutes of sexual favors. As always, the pretty girls were the ones in the most demand.

For the first couple of weeks, Natalia got hit on daily, even multiple times, but she made it evident that her plans there didn't include any of that type of behavior, free or not. After she made that very obvious, no one pressed or annoyed her about it anymore. Everyone knew that she was part of the world of education and had much higher values than most of the inmates there.

While she was almost like a psychologist to most of the

women, she always kept their secrets to herself. Many times, especially when a high profile inmate would come up to Natalia to talk, the guards would question her about that conversation later on. They would ask Natalia for information in a friendly way at first and then would pressure her to give them something they could use for gossip.

The times when Natalia couldn't help other inmates with something specific, she would give them another valuable thing: peace of mind. Natalia taught them how to look for the answers within their hearts and how to trust their intuition. She showed them how to use positive thinking and how to visualize their dreams as real as possible, every time they felt down or depressed. She explained to them how much of what they think and believe affects their mood and the outcome of their life.

Most of the issues they came to her with were related to missing their families and kids or regretting the crimes they had committed. Some of the women came to her for advice on personal life or relationships, in which Natalia didn't have much knowledge. In that type of a case, she would tell them to follow their gut feelings. She advised them to concentrate on their happiness and progress first and then on pleasing and doing things for others around them.

Since it was a medium security facility, it was easy for inmates to get mistreated without anyone noticing. Most of the abused were young and beautiful and usually not committed to other inmates. The younger and better-looking girls were those who got forced into inappropriate behavior, even by the guards, who used their authority to get what they wanted. Some of the guards paid the hottest and the most willing inmates for oral sex instead of forcing them into it.

One of the girls who came to Natalia confessed that two

of the guards paid her five rubles each for her to go down on them for a few minutes. She said that it was happening at the beginning of each of their work days. She told Natalia that unlike a lot of inmates there, she wasn't attracted to the same sex, but did perform oral sex to get the money.

Another young inmate told Natalia that no one had offered her any money and instead she was forced into it by one specific guard. She related to Natalia that the guard blackmailed her into sex by threatening to disclose to the other inmates, details about her crime which involved child abuse while under the influence of cocaine. That was a blatant no-no for the majority of the inmates there. It was understandable since most women there were mothers, sisters, and even grandmothers. They had a natural hatred towards the girls who abused their kids.

The only thing Natalia could do during those confessions was to teach other inmates how to pray and find the strength to live with whatever difficulties they were facing. Although Natalia's teachings sounded strange to most of the girls at the beginning of their talk, by the time they left, they felt happier and much more positive. Even if they didn't get the answer they were looking for, they got something far more valuable. She believed in them and made sure they trusted in themselves just as much. She told them that the real power was within every one of them and the rest would work itself out somehow, in some way. As long as they stayed truthful and loyal to their dreams they were going to be ok.

Her teachers and other employees all saw how much Natalia enjoyed helping others; but, they also noticed that after she finished both of her degrees, she started to get bored. There were no other classes that she needed to take, yet her need for growth made her anxious. The head professor decided to promote Natalia to a full-time teacher to make the girl feel useful. She wanted Natalia to grow even further.

The professor was an older, heavy-set woman, with a big swept-up hairdo and round glasses. She reminded everyone of a kind-hearted grandma that was waiting home waiting for them. Her cute looks didn't stop anyone from having tremendous respect for her. That particular professor was the one who ended up setting the meeting up with Natalia and the other professors. She was also the one who had the final say in Natalia's promotion and ended up approving it, giving Natalia her classroom and ability to teach mathematics full time.

It was like a breath of fresh air, and it gave her a nice boost of new energy and a feeling of being of service to others. She ended up being the favorite teacher of all the inmates there. The care with which she treated every single one of her students was more significant than what anyone had ever seen before. Natalia was indeed the most distinctive and caring teacher that prison ever had.

Ironically, just as in the past, Natalia had not met the prison's director yet, even though she had been there for almost four years. It was not a typical thing to spend time with the directors of any jails unless the inmate was in big trouble or on a rare occasion the opposite of that.

Now the time started to fly by even faster. Before Natalia knew it the day had come for her to get both of her official diplomas. She was finally going to have something tangible in her hands, like a fruit she had ripped off of the tree of knowledge that she had planted.

Natalia got called into the director's office. When she got there, the double doors were already wide open. It was Deja vu much like Natalia had experienced with her first meeting with Jana Vasilevna. Unlike before, this time she knew why she was going there and what she was about to receive.

The moment Natalia walked in, a smile naturally spread across her face. The room was full of people. To the left of her, she saw all of her teachers, professors, and a few other workers from the kitchen and the library. To the right side, there were a dozen guards and a couple of nurses with whom she often chatted. Everyone was looking at her with genuine happiness. A couple of teachers even had visible tears for the first time in their lives, because they saw an inmate graduate while still in prison. It was also the first time anyone there had earned double bachelor's degrees.

Natalia took a few steps forward and looked straight ahead to see the director right in front of her. She was delighted to meet her finally. This director also seemed surprisingly lovely.

Natalia also noticed a few similarities between this office and that of Jana Vasilevna. Some things here made her feel much more welcome. The sizeable triple window behind the main desk had a view of the beautiful green mountains. The window was so big that Natalia could even see a few dozen houses with smoke coming out of their chimneys. Overall the atmosphere was very cozy and warm.

Once again the warden was a woman. This one was a bit older but still beautiful. She was noticeably short and not more than five feet in height, even with high heels. She would catch anyone's attention anywhere she went. The director wore a black pantsuit. It was perfectly-pressed and tailored to her figure. Her black hair was short and tastefully styled with a modern bobbed haircut. She had beautiful brown eyes and thick, but perfectly shaped eyebrows. They accentuated the ideal proportions of her small face. She looked more like a doll than a human being. People would have to think hard if they tried to guess her age. It was almost impossible to believe that she was close to sixty years old. It was hard for Natalia to think that Jana Vasilevna was the warden of a maximum security prison. It was even more astonishing that this woman was also a warden.

"Good Morning, Natalia," she said with a smile.

"Good Morning, Mrs. Malenkova," replied Natalia, smiling at the director. There was a vase full of roses on the desk, and the aroma from the flowers was filling up the whole room, giving out a calm, peaceful aura. The bright red color of the flowers naturally shifted Natalia's attention to them right after her greeting.

"I see you like my beautiful flowers?"

"Yes, I do! They are beautiful!"

"There is always a bouquet of fresh flowers on my desk and also at home. I made that very clear to my husband on our first date! Here we are now, 35 years later, and I'm still inhaling the natural and calming aroma of my beautiful flowers."

"Wow, you can get something you asked for 35 years ago? I don't know how I could do that, but it surely is amazing!"

"Well, you are still young and can make that happen. I am going to give you a little piece of advice: something my mother told me when I finished college. Don't ever settle for less than what you deserve! Never, ever! You need to set your expectations high right off the bat and make sure that the man you pick knows not only how fortunate you are to have him but also how lucky he is that you have chosen him. Tell him that you want to be treated just as well, if not better, 20, 30, and even 40 years from the day of your first date! If you do that, your love will survive through it all. Trust me on that!"

"Thank you so much Mrs. Malenkova, that's precious advice. I'll make sure that I will tell my chosen one that I like my coffee early in the morning, served right after it gets brewed, so the aroma of it is still there!"

"You are too funny!" answered the director and the whole room filled with laughter from such a cute and straightforward personal requirement that Natalia shared. It was indeed magical to see everyone laughing and happy, especially on such a fantastic occasion.

The director picked up two diplomas from her desk and walked around the table to present them. As she walked up closer, it became apparent that she was a lot shorter than Natalia. It was also evident that her height didn't prevent her from being respected and valued by others.

"Here you are, sweetheart!" she addressed Natalia and handed her both of the diplomas.

It was an emotional moment for Natalia, and she felt positive vibes all around her. Everyone there was genuinely happy for her and everything that she accomplished.

"Thank you so much, Mrs. Malenkova. It means the world to me!" said Natalia with a grateful look as she tightly hugged both of her diplomas.

The director gave her a short, sincere hug and stepped back a little, leaving her hands on Natalia's shoulders.

"You know Natalia, Jana Vasilevna was so right about you! You are an extraordinary woman, and you are going to do great things during your lifetime! She also told me to tell you that she is very proud of you and that you shouldn't stop now!"

"Aww, I truly miss her! How is she doing? I wish I could see her again one day!"

"When you are free you can always go and visit! No one can stop you from that," answered the warden, walking back and around her desk.

"I definitely will," said Natalia while giving her diplomas a loving look. Just like her high school credentials, their covers where red leather. That was the color signifying high-honor graduates.

"Excuse me," asked Natalia. "I just realized that I didn't catch something you mentioned from Jana Vasilevna."

"Ok, what part of it are you referring to?"

"You stated that she said not to stop now? What does that mean? What am I supposed to continue with?"

"Well, what I think she meant is that you shouldn't stop getting your education and should continue moving up. I'm pretty sure that's what she was talking about."

"Ok, I understand. Unfortunately, it wouldn't work. I have already checked on that, and I'm only able to get to the bachelor degree level at this facility."

"That's correct, but who said you have to stay here?"

Natalia's eyes opened wide, and she paused. She was not sure what to say and couldn't find any words at that moment. The director was smiling, and her arms crossed: an unusual sight coming from a conservatively dressed woman. For a moment she reminded Natalia of a genie in a bottle, who came out with an attitude but was ready to make any wishes come true.

"Natalia, are you ok?" she asked while still smiling.

"Yes, yes, I am. I'm ok," answered the nervous girl.

"Ok, great. So what I was trying to say is that if you want to continue your education and earn a master's degree, you don't have to stay here at this facility!" She paused for a few seconds and then added, "You do want to get more education, right?"

"Me? Oh my God, yes, of cause I do! I would love to continue my education!" Her voice was shaky. She was only prepared to get her diplomas, and now she was shocked. The feeling of something huge that was about to happen was overwhelming her.

"That is great!" replied the director and turned towards her desk. She pushed a thin packet towards Natalia and looked up. "You are probably familiar with this process already, but still look it over. When you finish, I need you to sign right above my signature, right there." She opened the folder and pointed to her official stamp and the signature underneath it.

"Is this . . ?"

"Yes, it is! It's your transfer release. You are going to continue your education at the minimum security facility. If you sign it today, we will set up the transportation for tomorrow morning."

To say that Natalia was in complete shock would be an understatement. Even though she believed in positive thinking and her faith, this was still completely unexpected. Everything was happening so fast. The moment when she signed the transfer papers, another Déjà vu came into her mind. It was like a replay of her transfer from the maximum security prison to here; yet, this move was more powerful and essential to her. It brought her so much closer to freedom and the new life she always wanted.

The moment Natalia signed the papers everyone in the room started to clap. The guards were whistling, and a couple of the teachers were crying. Natalia was in too much shock to cry. She felt very humble, thankful and knew very well that every person in that room truly believed in her. She was becoming who she was always meant to be: a beautiful human being on the inside and the outside. Natalia had become a person who was using her unfortunate circumstances to better her life in every way.

"I am so grateful for your kindness. You don't know what this means to me," Natalia finally said out loud, addressing everyone in the room.

Everyone started to come up to her to give her hugs and kisses. It felt like she had won an Olympic Medal for running a hard 25K marathon with hundreds of roadblocks, and now her family was celebrating this win alongside her.

Things were unfolding like a fairy tale. Natalia was living a dream, and her prison sentence now looked more like a blessing. She was off the streets, getting an education, creating friends and helping others stay hopeful and focused.

The very next day she was transferred to a minimum security facility. She was the only inmate on the bus. It was much smaller and more comfortable than the previous ones she had been on before. Even though the trip took over a day, the driver stopped every few hours, and Natalia was able to go to the bathroom. She had full freedom of leaving the bus to go into the station. The guards just watched her from a few feet away. It was a strange feeling for Natalia to be able to walk around without her hands cuffed together.

When they finally arrived, and she saw the facility, it reminded her of one of the hotels that she was in during her time of working the streets. Now she didn't have anxiety or stress and was completely happy to be there.

This facility had no wires around it. The only thing that could give a hint that the bus had arrived at another prison was a tall, see-through fence and a gate with pillars. The plaque in the center of the entrance read "Minimum Security All Female Facility #3". The front door of this facility was locked 24/7, but no one ever tried to leave or escape from it. This minimum security prison was more like a college campus or a mini getaway. The majority of the girls who there were either homeless or worked the streets. For them to be there was more like a retreat. No one was in a rush to leave.

Natalia received a warm welcome. She also got a fully functioning room that looked more like a studio apartment. She started to teach the very next morning and fell in love with everyone there right off the bat.

Most of the girls at that facility were between eighteen years old and mid-twenties. From what she heard, they were serving short sentences for crimes like prostitution or stealing. Those were the girls with whom Natalia felt the most substantial connection. She had been in their spot and knew the lives they lived outside of these walls.

She was one of ten teachers there but became the favorite one within the first few days. All the girls loved her and behaved perfectly while in her classroom. About a week after Natalia started to teach, other teachers showed up to her class and sat there, observing the entire lesson. They wanted to see what she was doing that was so unique that made her students behave and pay attention. They didn't know that the answer was straightforward.

Natalia genuinely cared for and understood her students. She knew what they did to get there, why they did it, and how lonely they felt on the inside every single day. Natalia didn't treat them like regular students. She treated them like her sisters and as a family, with love and care. The inmates saw it, felt it, and indeed appreciated it. Their behavior and high grades in her class were the results of all that.

Two weeks after she got there, her classes and requirements for the master's degree also started. Professors from a couple of big-city universities began to come up to the facility specifically to teach her. They brought all the required material for Natalia to do her research and other assignments, so she could successfully earn a Master's Degree in Business and Accounting.

She was truly living a dream life, the kind she had never had and the kind that she had wished for during all of her hardships. Now, to be completely happy, all she needed was her little Nadia. She wondered every single night what her daughter might look like, where she was living, what kind of family her little girl was with or if she was struggling without her mother.

Another week later, to her surprise, she got the opportunity to meet the prison's director. It was a very casual meeting that Natalia was invited to right after the warden came back from her two-week vacation. Natalia didn't know what to expect but knew that most likely this warden was also a beautiful and classy woman.

To her amazement, this director was very different from the last two. It was not just because she was much younger [at most in her early 30s] but also because she looked like a rock star. She reminded Natalia of someone from a heavy metal rock band, and the first time in her life she was dressed more professionally than the director herself.

The warden was a very tall woman, dressed in black from head to toe. She had on tight black jeans, a sleeveless top, and very thick leather platform shoes. She had short, black, spiked hair that looked like a freshly-cut boy's haircut and heavy eye makeup that was the final touch making her look like a rock chick.

Their meeting reminded her of a school principal and a student, with Natalia being the principal who was reprimanding a girl for coming to class dressed inappropriately. It was quite humorous, but Natalia knew better than to judge people by their appearance. The director's attire didn't cloud Natalia's mind by any means. It was evident that this and all the other wardens were in their positions for a good reason. Natalia's responsibility was to respect them, even if they were wearing an outfit like a Mickey Mouse.

"Hey there, come right in," said the director as soon as Natalia showed up at her doorway.

"Good Morning, Mrs. Klasnova," answered Natalia and quickly walked over to the table.

"Please have a seat over there by the coffee table. I rarely use my desk. It's not comfortable and way too short for me. Oh, and please don't address me like that! I'm only ten years older than you, so just call me Alina."

"Ok, Alina, I appreciate your casual welcome!"

"My pleasure, hon, it's a pleasure to meet you."

"Oh, don't say that," answered Natalia. "I'm humbled to be able to meet you. I'm also happy to be able to contribute my knowledge to all the amazing girls living here."

"Well, they are surely an interesting bunch and unfortunately, believe it or not, most of them will be back here within a few days of their release. I tend to think they prefer to be here instead of in the outside world. I can't blame them much though."

"I guess I can see your point; but still, I will do my best to make them feel like they can do better than walking the streets or wasting their lives. They could be using their time serving themselves and others around them in productive and valuable ways."

"Thank you, Natalia! Thank you very much! You are a breath of fresh air, and I love your positive attitude. I hope that you can also get your Master's Degree here and that the next few years will go by for you in rewarding ways."

"Thank you so much, Alina. I'm very fortunate to have such great friends and amazing directors along my journey. I hope I can be of great service for you and everyone else here."

"Oh, don't you worry about that! I know how hard it is to

work and earn an education. I had a Master's Degree in Criminal Justice and worked my way through college the whole time, while my single mother worked two teaching jobs. I remember her working day and night while bringing home only a small amount of money. Believe it or not, there are two most underpaid professions in our country, and those are teachers and doctors. It's ridiculous how they both are the most vital to the society, and yet they are very much underpaid and completely underappreciated. Nevertheless, enough talk about that. Welcome and I hope you like your temporary but cozy home!"

They shook hands and spent a few more minutes chatting about life and things that they both enjoyed. Alina turned on her cassette player and put on her favorite classic rock group called "Queen." Natalia stayed there for a little longer and enjoyed every minute of their time together. It was the beginning of yet another real bond she was building and a small look at the outside world she was going to join very soon.

The time was flying by like a fast-forwarded movie, but Natalia still had three more years to serve. After only six short months she was able to earn her Master's Degree and yet again, receive her high-honors red diploma.

All of her professors, who taught at the two very prestigious business universities in Moscow, considered Natalia to be the most successful student they had ever had. She had something that the others didn't. She was hungry, hungry for success, freedom, education, and stability: the things that were going to help her to succeed and to have a great future.

Her outstanding performance and discipline month after month and year after year made her the topic of many conversations throughout different events in the business world. Her test scores and research papers were used as study material in many courses throughout the city of Moscow and the nearby regions. Her name was known to many, and knowledge of her abilities was spreading like wildfire.

She was only 24 and already well known in the business and educational world. By the end of 1997 and with all of her diplomas in hand, she was getting one job offer after another. Companies around the city and the country were trying to hire her ahead of time, knowing very well that she had another two and a half more years to serve. Luckily for Natalia, there was a federal law preventing companies and businesses from discriminating against a person's record. The only exception to that rule was a conviction for money laundering. It was her time to shine, and she couldn't wait to be able to do just that.

Her official release date was to be April 28, 2000, and so often Natalia thought about that time: a new decade, another century, and even a new millennium. She felt a bit scared that she went to prison in one millennium and was going to come out in the next one. Just the feeling of coming out into an unknown world was sticking in the back of her mind. On the other hand, Natalia felt excited that she was part of a different generation. She was one who was going to witness such a rare phenomenon as a transition from one millennium to the next. Not just ten years or one hundred, but a move into the next one thousand years. It felt like an honor to her.

She prayed every morning and night to God and the Universe for strength, guidance, and patience. She knew that her firm belief for a brighter future accounted for half of her success. There is a reason people give their all to prayers. If it comes from the depths of their hearts, then whatever they ask for is going to be granted, somehow and in some way.

At the end of December, a couple of weeks after Natalia

received her Master' Degree, she got called into the director's office. It was a Friday night, around 8 p.m., way past the time when Alina usually worked.

"Good Evening Alina, you asked for me?" said Natalia, catching her breath from walking rapidly through the facility.

"Yes. Hi! Please come in," Alina answered. She sounded intriguingly excited.

"Thanks! You are working late tonight! Is everything ok?"

"Is everything ok?" The director smiled. "Everything is great! I was just waiting for the results from something I have been working on for a couple of months now. I stayed late, knowing that I was going to find out the outcome of it at some point this afternoon. Then, I knew I would need to do a few other things to complete the paperwork, so here I am."

"Oh really, and what was it you were working on?"

"Well, obviously it has to do with you, which I'm sure you already guessed by now. Why else would I call you in?" They smiled at each other and then laughed out loud. The apparent point Alina just made was too funny to pass over.

"OK, I'm going to tell you this right out, and I hope you don't get upset because I didn't tell you about it before."

"Ok, no worries. I won't be mad. Go ahead."

"Well, I have filed for your parole, and I've asked the court to give you an early release from here, because of your accomplishments and exemplary behavior."

"Excuse me? Can you say that again? You did what?"

"I filled out the legal paperwork and asked the court to shorten your sentence by two and half years and set you free!"

"What do you mean free? Like I will be able to leave and get my place and work a regular job? Free like that?"

"Yes," said Alina and smiled. Her eyes were watery.

Natalia started to feel light-headed and had to sit down so

she wouldn't fall. She wasn't sure how to react to what she just heard or if she should even believe it. It just sounded way too unreal. It was one thing to get transferred from prison to prison, but this was different and not realistic. Natalia just stood there in silence, staring at Alina.

"Are you ok? You look pale. Did I upset you or something?"

Natalia was too shocked and confused even to reply. It wasn't just about the possibility of being released from prison two and a half years earlier. It was about knowing that someone she had met only a few months back would do something like this for her.

A minute later, Natalia broke the silence and asked, "So, what was the outcome of your request Alina?" Her gentle voice was shaky, and her words were so quiet that Alina could hardly hear them.

"They granted it. The court gave you an early release, Natalia. They don't even need your testimony. It's all set and done. As of 6 a.m. tomorrow morning you are completely free to leave."

Natalia froze up again, and for the first time in many years, tears of happiness started to flow down her face uncontrollably. She wasn't moving or even blinking. She didn't look like she was still breathing. What Alina had just said was also not a part of Natalia's wildest imagination.

"I know you are surprised, but we both know that you truly deserve this! You are amazing! Hear me! You are amazing! Remember that," Alina shouted with emotion and moved closer to Natalia. The poor girl still had zero reaction. She was trying to figure out if this was a dream or some kind of a cruel joke that Alina was playing on her.

"Oh! There is one more thing that we have to do, and I need your participation in it. You need to decide where you are going to work. It's something that the judge requires us to set up for any of the offers you have received, and I believe you have over twelve to review. From what I have checked out, they are all offering you an apartment in the center of Moscow and a sign-on bonus equal to your first six months pay. I even saw a couple of offers that included a brand new company car!"

Natalia was getting more and more overwhelmed with every word she was hearing. Meanwhile, Alina poured herself a cup of hot coffee and sat down in the comfortable reclining chair across from Natalia. She took off her shoes and settled into a comfortable position. "So, are you going to stare at me or can we start looking through the list? I would love to help you pick your first paying job. I'm good at that!" Natalia was still not responding. Alina was smiling. She understood Natalia's numbness about what was happening. The director knew that she had just changed this girl's life in ways that no one had ever done before. She was acting calm, but inside she wanted to cry and hug Natalia like they just went through the war side by side and won it.

Natalia stayed frozen for a few more minutes while Alina slowly sipped on her hot coffee, gently blowing into the cup every few seconds. Finally, Natalia spoke up without moving her eyes off Alina's face.

"Alina?"

"Yes?"

"How did you do this? Why? When? Is it true? Am I free?"

"Yes, it's true! Of course, it's true! Do you think I would joke about that?" playfully laughed Alina.

"I am lost for words! I still can't believe you did that for me! I don't even know how to repay you. You are an angel, sent to me by God." Natalia started to cry. She was touched and overwhelmed by Alina's good deed.

"Honey, you owe me nothing, absolutely nothing. I wanted to do it for you because it was the right thing to do. Now, you can start living your life to the fullest and find her." She smiled.

They both understood what she was talking about without any specifics. Those were not needed. Alina read Natalia's record and knew what she did to get her sentence.

A moment later Natalia glanced at the window and saw a full moon, slowly rising in the sky. It reminded her of the ride in the trunk of that BMW with her daughter and how the moon tried giving her as much light as it could so they weren't scared. Now years later, that same planet was witnessing another life-changing moment in Natalia's life, this time for the best.

Natalia snapped back to reality, and now, with a fully returned attention, she moved her seat closer to Alina. They started to look through the stack of offers and shortly after that agreed on the same one. This company and what they were offering matched Natalia's needs and the schedule she desired. It was a big financial firm that operated all over the country, and Natalia's position would be a regional controller. She was going to travel most of her week throughout Moscow and the neighboring regions. She was going to help the client get financially compliant and ready for any audits by the different government organizations. It was perfect, exactly what she wanted and her salary was going to be way above the average rate.

Just as expected, the moment Alina called the company they both had chosen, the president of it was beside himself. He was lucky, and he knew it. The man assured Alina that Natalia would be adequately taken care of and said that his chauffeur would be there at eight o'clock the next morning. He provided her the address of Natalia's new apartment and all the other things required by the court and prison information for a successful release.

Sure enough, at precisely 8 a.m. the next day, Natalia was ready to go, saying her goodbyes to all the inmates, her students, and all the guards and workers she had grown to love. When Natalia finally walked up to the front door of the prison, Alina gave her the signed papers for release and then unlocked the door. Together, they walked out and started to make their way towards the front gate. It was already open, waiting for Natalia to cross the line into freedom. The poor girl was looking up at the sky, trying to comprehend that she didn't have to go back inside ever again. Meanwhile, Alina couldn't control the tears streaming down her face, and she kept wiping them off as fast as she could so others wouldn't notice. There was no denying that she and Natalia had developed a powerful bond.

The moment they came up to the open gate, Alina grabbed Natalia and pulled her close, giving her a tight hug and placing a loving kiss on her forehead. It resembled a goodbye that an older sister might be saying to her younger sibling who was leaving home for good.

"Please don't forget us. Write and call. I am not going anywhere, and I'll be here if you need me. Please let me know how you are doing with your the new job and how life is treating you overall. My wish is for you to find and reunite with your little girl very soon! Now, please go, I'm not going to say goodbye."

Natalia was emotional as well but was so eager to step over that line of freedom that she couldn't bear to wait anymore.

"I will never, ever forget what you have done for me! You are an amazing friend, and your kindness will come back to you in multiple ways. I know it! It always does!"

Natalia took a deep breath and looked at the white line on

the ground at the gate's entrance. She stepped right over it and into freedom. She turned her head back, looked at Alina and smiled. It was a silent and final goodbye. At this point, the words between them were unneeded.

The white Mercedes was waiting for Natalia just a few steps ahead. The chauffeur had already opened the front passenger door and was waiting for Natalia to walk up. As she got in the car, she realized that a brand new life was about to unfold right in front of her. Natalia was still humble and now knew for sure that her happiness was just around the corner. Natalia hesitated for a split moment, but deep inside she was ready. She had paid her dues in full to prisons and society.

The car moved and slowly disappeared down the long, dusty road, leaving behind a cloud of painful but life-changing memories of her time in prison.

VERONIKA GASPARYAN

CHAPTER SEVEN

Even though orphanages had plenty of donated toys during the holiday season, children were never pleased. They craved much more. They wanted parents, a family dinner and a Christmas tree with wrapped presents under it.

Children under thirteen who were part of the state system were living in different orphanages around the country. Kids thirteen and older were mostly in foster homes, with both or just one adult living there. On the rare occasion when no foster care parents were available, even the thirteen-year-old kids had to live in the orphanages. No matter where the children were, it was just not the happiest of situations.

Most of the orphanages were in pretty good condition, and there were many people on the staff including a director, teachers, a night shift nanny, and even a nurse. The ages for children were anywhere from a few days old to teenagers.

The kids at most of the orphanages were cared for very well. They were appropriately dressed for the season, took showers a few times a week and had meals three times per day. They were also getting the same education as any child would at a regular school. A lot of different local and nearby organizations and regional governments donated food, clothing, and supplies. During the holiday season, those donations also included games and toys for both girls and boys.

The ratio between younger and older kids in any given orphanage was never even. The newborns and toddlers were adapted much more often than the older kids. It was understandable. The majority of people didn't want to deal with kids who already had established personalities and habits.

With the toys being the most significant part of the holiday donations and board games being a smaller percentage, the older kids had to learn to share. On some occasions, they would quietly take or openly grab the toys out of the youngsters' hands. Then the rooms would be filled with crying, screaming, arguing and even fighting.

Although there were lots of gifts and things to play with, it was never precisely enough for every single child. Teachers and caregivers organized, sorted, and gave out the toys to the best of their abilities. It still doesn't mean that every individual child ended up with his or her desired or age-appropriate present.

If that wasn't bad enough, each orphanage always had that one child who still ended up empty-handed. That child would usually be known as a troublemaker; and therefore, even during the holidays, the teachers seldom tried to look out for him or her.

Most of the orphanages had two groups of kids. Some of the more prominent locations had three. The most common division had a group of newborns and kids up to around five years old. Another section had six-year-olds and up. In some cases, the older kids coming from abusive homes and neglectful parents were already emotionally unstable. In other cases, some children had been there since they were newborns.

The overall environment for teachers wasn't relaxed. Some of them worked in an orphanage their whole working lives and became emotionally attached to the kids. Favoritism became inevitable. Even with that, they had to discipline those who misbehaved. Most of the time those kids were older. The punishments usually included a timeout, no playing outside and no TV time when the group watched cartoons. Physical abuse wasn't standard practice, and yet a few slaps on the butt for more serious things like stealing or abusing others was considered a fair discipline.

Because the teachers faced a somewhat hard environment and long work days, in recent years the government made some changes to their work schedules and added more positions to each orphanage. Now, instead of one, there were two shifts for the teachers, and during the night there were two or three nannies instead of just one, who was sleeping there. A secretary was also added to assist directors with all the paperwork instead of the teachers having to do it.

Privacy of information about each child was a big deal. The only two people who knew anything about the kids were the director and his secretary. The director had one of the two keys to the files that were inside of a metal filing cabinet in the director's office, and only he had full access to it. A second key was with the child services of the city of Moscow. The only time it was needed was on that rare occasion when a director had lost or misplaced his copy.

Despite all the precautions taken to keep the information safe, the complete privacy of information about the children was almost impossible. The secretary that was now involved with some of the paperwork didn't take the privacy laws as seriously as the director did. Gossip and slipped information were highly possible.

The majority of the orphanages were on the outskirts of the major cities, and only a few were within central Moscow. In the center itself, there were only about fifteen locations, and that number was not significant. Considering that Moscow has over twelve million people living there and is the biggest city in the whole country, fifteen orphanages is below the standard. For that size of the area and so many people living there, Moscow should have at least 100 of them.

The technical and business-oriented general population seemed to dislike having orphanages around them. The big issue of child welfare right under their noses would force them to pay more attention to it. It was much easier to ignore if it was not there to see.

With that, most of the orphanages were built and located on the outskirts of the city, as well as nearby villages and regions. All of the locations had cute titles. The names usually had something to do with a flower, a tree, or with water. It would make a little more sense if their names had something to do with winter or snow. That whole region had a significant amount of snowfalls. The roofs of the orphanages were covered in snow for at least several months each year. You would think that names like Snowflake, Snowman or even Santa's Angels would match much better.

One of those orphanages with an odd name was a smaller one in the Pavlovo village, a couple of hours away from the very center of Moscow. It was called "Daisy" and was actually in one of the colder areas of the region. This village and a few others nearby usually got three to four feet of snow during each of the regular snowstorms. During those snowfalls, kids were not even allowed to go outside and play until some of the snow melted, and temperatures were at least above zero. No one wanted the kids to get sick, freeze, or possibly get lost and stuck in the high snowbanks around the yard.

Everyone who worked there was accommodating. The director was kind, the teachers were patient, and the nurse was caring. Even the night shift nannies were attentive and took good care of all the kids. The interior and exterior of the orphanage looked pleasant, and the staff made sure everything was clean.

The doors of Daisy were always locked, and the visitors or people who brought donations had to ring the doorbell. Of course, the locks weren't new, just like the majority of the doors and windows, but they still worked. It was not easy to pick a lock to escape, at least not for the kids. Plus, no one wanted to go outside into the freezing air in the first place - almost no one.

As in every school and daycare around the world, there was always that one child, who would stand out from the crowd and most of the time not in an excellent way. The Daisy orphanage was not an exception to that rule.

"Eugene Petrovich, may I come in please?" a worried teacher knocked on the director's door and asked.

"Yes, Elena Stepanova, come on in," he answered.

The door quickly opened, and a short, heavy-set woman in her late 50's promptly walked in. She looked distraught.

"Have a seat. You look pale. Here, take a shot of vodka. It should calm you down!"

The teacher grabbed the already full shot glass from the director's hand and hurriedly drank it down. She shuddered a few times because, for her, the Stolichnaya vodka was too strong. Then she placed the empty glass on the director's desk and sat down, taking a deep breath. She wanted to have enough air for the explanation she was about to give to her boss.

"Mr. Petrovich, it's that girl again! It's Nadia! She is going to get the best of all of us! You have to do something about her. She ran away again, and this time it's freezing outside with up to three feet of snow. A few of us have already looked everywhere. We even looked in the basement, and still nothing. The front door was originally locked, and now it's not," the teacher said so fast that she had to stop and breathe for a few seconds. The director was looking more and more nervous.

"Again? What is wrong with that kid?" he yelled out and smacked his desk with his hand. "Why does she keep running away? To where? To whom? Never mind all that. How did she open that lock? Didn't we just have it fixed a week ago?"

"Mr. Petrovich, she is just way too energetic and sneaky for us. Every time she wants to get out of here she waits until all the other kids are taking an afternoon nap and we are all in the kitchen eating lunch. That's when she quietly and quickly sneaks out. I mean, yes, we always end up finding her at the train station, but it is still way too much stress for all of us. It is also a bad example for the younger kids. Can you please do something about it?"

"Wait, what about the snow? That didn't stop her? I don't understand. I just don't understand. I mean, we treat her so well here, and she is still ungrateful and unappreciative!" the director paused and looked down at the floor. "Oh and what about that weird old doll she carries around? Did she take her, too?"

"Yes, she did. She always takes that thing with her. I don't know what is wrong with that girl, and no, of course, the snow didn't stop her. Nothing seems to stop her. It can be the hottest day of the year or below zero, and she still runs away. We are just too tired of it, way too tired."

"Hmmm, I understand your point here. I guess I will have to look into transferring Nadia elsewhere. It surely would be a shame. She has been with us since she was a newborn. Have you ever asked her why she keeps running away and why to the train station?"

"Yes, of course, we did. We spoke about that to Nadia numerous times, and her answer is always the same. She says that she is too smart to stay with all the kids here and she wants to go to the big city and become an actress, plain and simple."

"Ok, well, you see now why I always say that it's bad for kids to watch TV? That's where they get those crazy ideas. They aren't content in wanting to be good wives and mothers when they grow up. They want to be famous, go places and do things. What is happening to this world? It's depressing, but anyway, enough of talking. Let's find her. Didn't you say she always goes to the train station?"

"Yes, Mr. Petrovich, she does, but she can't get on the train itself without a ticket. In the past, we caught up with her right when she arrived at the station. Today though, a lot longer time had gone by before we realized she was missing. We should probably leave right now."

"Yes, let's go. I will call the station and notify them, just in case Nadia shows up there before we do. Hopefully, there is still someone there."

"Ok, try calling them. I hope the poor thing isn't going to freeze or get lost on the way there. She has never run away during such cold temperatures, especially with the snowstorms like we had for the past two weeks. That crazy girl!"

"Ok. Well, Elena put your boots and coat on quickly. As far as

I know the last train leaves at 8 p.m. so there should be plenty of people at the train station who will notice a little girl alone. Let's get going. The roads are going to be hard to drive on."

The snow had been falling steadily for over a week, and it was not easy for people to keep up with it. Thick fluffy snow was covering all the cars, side streets, and roofs of the buildings. It looked like nature's white fuzzy blanket, covering everything from head to toe.

The only way for the director and the teacher to get to the train station before 8 p.m. was to take an old jeep belonging to one of the teachers. She didn't mind at all because it was evident that they had a situation on their hands which needed a resolution as soon as possible.

The director went outside first. As soon as he saw the conditions, he realized that the next hour was going to be very difficult and nerve-racking. He turned on the jeep to warm it up and started to clean the snow off the roof and the windows. The teacher was still putting on her furry snow boots and mumbling things under her breath. It was apparent she wasn't having a good day.

By now, the other teachers had brought all the kids into the main playroom, so they wouldn't know what was happening. Of course, most of the older kids already figured out that Nadia had run away again. Still, no one was talking about it or asking any questions. Most of the kids in any given orphanage had gotten brainwashed from the day they arrived. They were told numerous times to mind their own business and to believe only what adults tell them.

Eugene Petrovich did his best to clean off as much snow as he could, and when he finished, he ran back into the building. He quickly went into his office to make the call to the train station. The only phone available at Daisy was the landline in this room. No one answered. Most of the workers had gone home, and the ticket windows closed no later than 6 p.m. especially during the winter. Now, it was 7:20. The only station employees who would possibly be there yet were the cleaning crew or the guards who usually came to work between 8 and 9 p.m.

The train station also had plenty of people in the waiting area. They usually got on the last train of the day. Those people were mostly residences of the village of Pavlovo and who worked night shifts in the center of Moscow. The majority of them worked as street cleaners, night guards or nannies. The town only had a little over five hundred residents living there, and local job openings were a rare thing to see.

Meanwhile, the brave and near-freezing little Nadia made her way through the cold dark roads and into the station. It took her over 6 hours, but she made it. Hungry, wet, tired and nervous she walked into the waiting area and looked around. The whole place had at least a couple of dozen people there. All but one of the seats was full. The bench that had one small available spot open was at the end of the room. Nadia headed straight towards it.

When she came closer to the bench, she realized that a man was sleeping on it. Even though he was tall, he was curled up to keep warm, so he covered only about three-quarters of the seating space. Most of the benches for the passengers were on the inside of the building. That was great, but freezing air was still able to get in because of the opening at the top of the steep stairway.

The good news was that Nadia had enough room to sit down and she did so, quietly and carefully. As soon as she settled into her spot, a sense of accomplishment filled her mind, so she took a deep breath and closed her eyes. Nadia knew very well that even though she had made it that far, it would only be a few minutes before someone would catch her and bring her back to Daisy. Still, despite it being hopeless, Nadia was happy that she accomplished another brave attempt to run away. At that point, the tired little girl just wanted to rest.

The minute she started to drift off to sleep, the man next to her began to snore. She opened her eyes and turned her head. Little Nadia was curious. She couldn't help it, so she got up and took a couple of steps towards him, carefully looking him over.

He was an older gentleman, dressed warmly. A furry Ushanka hat was covering his head and ears, and his thick winter jacket was zipped all the way up. What he was wearing was not what caught her attention. What she saw was the half-empty bottle of vodka on the floor next to him and a pack of Marlboro cigarettes he was clutching in his hands. Still, to her, it all looked very entertaining.

The open bottle of vodka was something that Nadia used to see on the desk of the director's office. Nadia was there quite often, as she was the most misbehaved child at the orphanage. The director always used to say, "Nadia, why are you staring at the bottle? I'm not an alcoholic. I am just a little cold, and I drink to stay warm." She figured the man on the bench was also trying to stay warm but had a little too much to drink.

Nadia came up close to the man's face and smiled. His strange snore and the sounds he was making were something in between humming and whistling. It was very rhythmic, almost like the sound of train wheels from one of the cartoons she saw on TV.

A few moments later the man started to get louder, or at least that's what Nadia thought. It was getting noisier, but it was not coming from the man. It was coming from every corner of the train station.

The sound was getting louder, and people were getting off the benches. Some were already making their way to the stairs that led to an outside platform. It was clear to Nadia now that the sound she was hearing was the approaching train. It was a massive, powerful train: the kind she saw in children's books, but never in real life. She paused for a moment to make sure that what she was hearing was, in fact, the train and when she was sure, Nadia got super excited.

"It's a train! Mister! Mister! It's a real train! Oh my God! It is a real moving train!" She started to scream with excitement and jumped up and down as if she had just seen the most beautiful doll in the world. The sleeping man didn't even blink.

Nadia wasn't stupid and knew that the guy was there to take that same train. There was no other reason to be sleeping at the station at this hour. Being a kind and caring girl, she squatted down and decided to wake him up. She didn't' want him to miss his train because she reasoned that he might be going somewhere important.

"Wake up, mister. The train is here! It will leave without you if you don't get up. Hello!"

She rocked him back and forth and repeated herself time after time. Meanwhile, all the other people had already made it to the top of the platform. She and the sleeping man were the only ones left. Nadia tried a few more times to wake him, but no matter what she did, he was not even moving. Nadia didn't know what else to do.

A second later the train engineer sounded a loud horn. It was the first out of the three blasts the train made before it left the station. Nadia shook the man even harder, but he still was not waking up. She decided to try one more time and then leave him alone. She did, and as she pushed his body one more time, something small fell out of his coat pocket.

It landed on the ground right next to her feet. Nadia looked down and saw a thick piece of paper with numbers and words printed all over it. Nadia picked it up and brought it close to her eyes. As she read the words written on it, it became very apparent. It was a train ticket from Pavlovo to the Central Moscow Train Station. It was for the train that was going to leave at any minute. Without thinking about what she was doing or how her next move was going to affect the rest of her life, little Nadia put the ticket into her coat pocket and got up. She thanked the man that was still in a deep sleep and started to run towards the main stairs.

Although she loved to run around and was the fastest child at Daisy, now she was running faster than ever before. It was the most important run of her life: the one that had to do with her freedom, even though the unknown was terrifying as well. Nadia was skipping two and even three steps at a time. She was going as fast as she could go because she was determined to get to the platform and on that train before it left.

When she got almost to the top of the stairs, she heard the second loud signal from the train pierce the air. She didn't stop. It was not an option. She had to keep going.

The moment she got up to the train platform, she ended up ten feet away from the train track and the actual train. Car number one was further out to the right of her, and the rest of the train was on the left. The car in front of her had a large number three on the side of the open door, and a tall, uniformed woman was standing in the doorway. Scared little Nadia stopped and looked directly at the woman.

"Hey you, are you getting on or what? We are about to leave! Why did you even leave the train? Kids shouldn't get out at the different stations without their parents. You could get kidnapped!

Hello? What are you standing there for, let's go?" screamed the woman at little Nadia who just stood there.

Thankfully, a second later, Nadia snapped out of it and said, "Yes, Ma'am. Yes, I am from this train, and my parents are inside. I was just checking the station out." Nadia bravely walked up to the door, grabbed the conductor's outstretched hand and was pulled onto the train.

"You kids just never listen! Children from your generation do whatever they want! Go to your parents, and I don't want to see you roaming the train until the next and final stop in two hours. Now go!" the woman said and gently pushed Nadia towards the door leading into the passenger compartment of the third car.

Without any hesitation, Nadia pushed open the door and walked inside. There were quite a few people there, but she did not want to stop or look at anyone. The last thing the poor girl needed was to be recognized and brought back to Daisy. Nadia looked down and then started to walk. She wanted to find an empty car or one with the least amount of passengers in it.

When she got to the end of car number three, the door on the other end opened and the conductor walked in. The nervous little girl quickly exited the car and ended up in the small space that was connecting two of them. She noticed how loud and shaky it was there. She could even see large wheels under the connected tiles of the floor. The mighty wheels were so noisy that it made Nadia feel overwhelmed; and yet at the same time, she felt the power contained in them. They could bring passengers to known and unknown destinations.

The curious girl looked to the side and saw the thick doors with the double glass inserts. It was scary to stand in that section, but she was curious. She took a couple of steps to the left and held on to the large handle on the door. It was darker on the inside than the outside. Snow covered every inch of the ground. The moonlight reflected on the trees creating silhouettes that looked like sleeping people.

The train station was long gone, and by now even the smaller houses had disappeared. They were out of sight. A winter wonderland appeared wherever she looked. "Thank you, God!" she whispered to herself, as she pressed her little forehead against the cold window. "You do exist," she said and smiled. The window she had her face against, began to fog up and a few seconds later it was hard to look through it. She took a couple of steps away from the outside door and walked towards the next car.

All the entry and exit doors of the cars had a thin glass insert in them. Some of those had curtains on them, and a few didn't. Nadia couldn't see what was in the next car, but as soon as she walked in, the unusually warm air caught her by surprise. It even smelled delicious, just like dinner time at her orphanage. It was a dining car that most of the passenger trains were required to have.

The moment she closed the door behind her, she looked the car over. It was now a habit she developed. There were a few square tables on each side and a corner bar all the way at the end on the right. The waitress behind it was carefully pouring hot coffee into a few cups she had prepared. She didn't even look up.

Nadia decided she had a few minutes to check out the rest of the car, so she looked to the right and saw a young couple holding hands at one of the tables. The man and woman were whispering something to each other. It reminded her of a funny scene from Tom and Jerry when Tom was trying to tell the pretty dressed-up kitty that he loved her. Nadia smiled and looked to the left.

She saw a big family with two parents at one table and three kids at the table right behind them. They were all still eating their dinner, and that's precisely what hungry Nadia smelled as soon as she got in that car. A second later she realized that she had spent too much time observing and needed to keep moving.

Nadia knew that none of those people were from Pavlovo or even any nearby villages for that matter. They were just way too well-dressed to be from anywhere other than the big city. They were probably going to check out Moscow and visit the Red Square or the Clock Tower. Those were always fascinating things, a family or a young couple could do.

She moved her attention back to the floor and started to move forward. She had no idea how many more cars there were on that train, but she figured there must have been a few. When she first saw the train, the end of it was not even visible, so there had to be at least half a dozen more cars after the dining car.

Meanwhile, the director and the teacher finally made it to the barely shoveled-out parking lot of the train station. They were at least a few minutes too late but didn't know it quite yet. When they walked into the waiting area, they realized that there was no one there except one man, who was sleeping on the farthest bench. They got very nervous and started to panic.

"Hurry, Elena, hurry. She must be with the others up there on the train platform."

Both of them rushed towards the stairs and ran up them as fast as their legs would allow them to go. When they finally made it the top, they stopped, trying hard to catch their breath. They saw that the platform was empty and there were no signs of the train. It was long gone. Of course, there were also dozens upon dozens of fresh footprints all around them, but they didn't think of looking down at the ground.

"We are too late, Mr. Petrovich. We are too late," said the teacher sadly. "She is gone now. She must have made it on the last train somehow. What are we going to do? How will we explain this to the board?" The teacher put her hands on her face and covered her eyes. She was scared for Nadia, but she was also scared that she was going to lose her job.

"No one can get on the train without a ticket," said a guy, who came around the corner after emptying out garbage containers on the platform. The director turned around and looked at the teacher with scared eyes.

"She must not have made it to the station. You said she has never run away in the snow before, so what if she got lost or hurt and is freezing on some side road right now? We need to find her. She must be somewhere between here and Daisy!"

"You are right, Mr. Petrovich, you are right. Let's find her. Let's also call the police station. Maybe there is someone there. They know the village better than anyone and can help."

They turned around and headed back down the stairs and out to the parking lot. All they had to do was just pay a little more attention to the details around them. If they had, they would have seen Nadia's small footprints in the same exact spot where they were standing. Those little prints were going towards the train; the train that left only a few minutes earlier. Ironically, they did not believe that she was capable of such a creative escape and that's where they lost, and she won.

CHAPTER EIGHT

Natalia was lying across two seats on the very last row of car number eleven. That day, she had worked from 6 a.m. to 4 p.m., and she was exhausted. Between work and travel that she did every single week, sleeping on the train was her usual thing.

For the past few days, Natalia was conducting a financial audit for one of the clients of the company for whom she worked. Unlike most of the auditors, Natalia liked her job. It wasn't as exciting as other professions would be, but she loved working with the numbers.

Despite the extensive travel, which made her the most tired, Natalia didn't mind being on the train. To most of her co-workers, that side of her job was a huge turn off but not for her. It was the opposite.

For the past two years, she had been traveling all over the region conducting audits and doing training for upper management in finances, accounting, and business. Indeed, during some weeks she spent 20 plus hours on trains, but she never complained about it. What she was doing now was nothing in comparison to what she was forced to do as a teenager.

Natalia was the one who asked for that particular position. She was very well aware of the extensive traveling, and to her, the more hours she spent away from the center of Moscow, the better. There were just too many bad memories that Natalia connected to the inner city. If she were to work locally, the chance of her meeting one of her clientele from her past was way too high. It wasn't worth it, even if it meant her wasting her precious time riding uncomfortable trains.

Natalia made the best of it and figured out a way to relax, even during the long rides. She always chose the last car of any of the trains she rode because the majority of those had double rows in their second half. Those double rows were perfect for parents who were traveling with children or passengers who needed much more space. Most of the time, Natalia either napped, lying down across two of the seats or put her legs up while working on her laptop.

After the last stop at Pavlovo, knowing that there were no more stations until reaching central Moscow, tired Natalia decided to take a nap. She stretched across the aisle seat and the window one next to her and closed her eyes. The rhythmic sound of the wheels as the train gained full speed, rocked her to sleep.

The same was true for the majority of the passengers on that train but not for little Nadia. She couldn't rest just yet. She was exhausted but on a mission of searching for an empty car. She was continuing her journey, moving steadily from one car to the next. The conductor seemed always to be only a couple of minutes behind her. Every time Nadia closed the door of the car she had just gone through, she heard the annoying and ear-piercing voice.

"Tickets, please, prepare your tickets. Hold them up if I have already stamped them! Tickets, please. Prepare your tickets."

The good news for Nadia was that as she was passing through each new car, there seemed to be fewer passengers. By the time she was almost at the end of the train, there were only about ten people in each car. She wasn't going to give up her search.

Nadia closed the door of car number ten and walked up to the next car. Before she looked through the glass insert to check the inside, Nadia looked up and saw the sign that read "YOU ARE ENTERING THE LAST CAR." She realized that it was the end of the train, and now she had no choice but to find the best spot in which to settle down. When she peered through the glass, she didn't see anyone in there. Happily, she pushed open the door and walked right in. The annoying sound of the conductor entering car number ten, followed immediately after.

Little Nadia carefully closed the door behind her and started to walk towards the middle section of that car. She saw that the regular seating rows with two on each side only went as far as the center. When she got to the last of those single rows, she sat down in the aisle seat on the right.

It was sad that in Nadia's naïve mind, she didn't realize that the conductor would eventually make her way into that car. Despite all of her attempts to stay away from people, she would have to face that woman sooner or later. She wasn't able to comprehend what would happen when the conductor caught up with her.

Nadia was well aware that young children couldn't travel without an adult or supervision by the conductor. Still, even now, she was too tired to think about it. She just wanted to be left alone and to sleep, even for just a little bit.

The tired little girl pulled her feet underneath her, put her doll inside of her coat and got as cozy as she could get. She was still short, and her head wasn't even visible above the seat. There was always a chance that the conductor could just check the car through the window and walk away. Unfortunately, that is not what happened, and Nadia was only able to rest for a moment.

"Tickets, please. Prepare your tickets or hold them up if I have stamped them already. Tickets, please prepare your tickets." The conductor was on auto-pilot and entered the last car without checking it out through the glass first.

If not for her ear-piercing announcement, which could probably wake up passengers in the previous two cars, most likely she wouldn't have awakened Natalia. Unfortunately, the sound was so loud that Natalia bolted upright in her seat the moment the conductor walked in. The noise and waking up so abruptly gave Natalia an immediate headache. She pressed her temples with both hands to release the pressure and pulled her head back.

The fresh memory of her dream was still there, but a massive migraine was making that memory disappear faster than Natalia wanted it to go. It was a good dream of her sitting on the porch of a beautiful lakeside house, reading a book that she had just finished writing. Natalia recalled hearing melodic sounds of birds singing in the nearby trees and the feeling of warmth from the summer sun beating down on her shoulders. Then, it was all gone as if she hadn't even dreamed it. Unlike the usual nightmares she had, that was the first beautiful dream that came to her in many years. The unfortunate young woman could not enjoy it to its fullest, and that made her bit mad.

The same conductor had checked her ticket three separate times since she boarded that train a few hours back. Now there she was screaming out that annoying phrase that Natalia already knew verbatim. On top of being loud, she was again moving towards the end of the car to check her ticket.

Irritated and still tired, Natalia started to search through her purse for the ticket with one hand while still holding her pounding forehead with the other one. Anyone else on that train by now would have snapped at the conductor, but not Natalia. She was just not the type to do that. She was too patient and too polite.

Meanwhile, scared little Nadia was pretending to be asleep. She was holding her doll as if it were the only thing she had. Her pretense did not work as well as she was hoping for and as soon as the conductor approached that row Nadia realized that her acting was about to be exposed.

"What are you doing here? You are the girl from the last station! I recognize you! You got back on the train a minute before we left. Wake up. Where are your parents?"

The woman was loud. It was apparent that she was trying to wake Nadia, assuming that the girl was asleep. Nadia had no choice but to open her eyes while still playing the role of a newly-awakened child. The girl was trying to act surprised and pretended to yawn.

"Oh, hello ma'am. Here is my ticket," said Nadia politely and pulled the ticket out of her coat pocket, showing it off like a lottery prize.

"Ok, so? It's not about the ticket! Why are you sleeping over here in the last car? You told me that your parents are on this train, so where exactly are they?"

Not knowing what to say, Nadia put down her head and paused. The conductor was staring at her, impatiently waiting for a response. Scared Nadia had to come up with something, so she said the first thing that came to her mind.

"Well, I didn't tell you everything correctly. My dad got me the ticket from Pavlovo, but then he had to go to work. He told me to stay in the waiting area until I heard the train and then go up to the platform. That's what I did." Nadia looked up, feeling confident in her story-telling abilities so far. Then she continued. "My mother is going to meet me at the train station in Moscow. They arranged all that between them." Nadia knew that she was probably in trouble, but she wasn't going to stop trying now. It wasn't the first time she did something she wasn't supposed to do.

"OH MY GOD!" screamed the conductor holding her head. "I am going to lose my job if anyone finds this out. You can't ride the train alone without special arrangements or an adult. What am I going to do?" The conductor looked like she was about to cry. It was not something that had ever happened to her during the twenty plus years she worked on the different trains. She looked back at Nadia, and as if it made a difference at that moment, she asked. "How old are you?"

"I am ten and a half," proudly answered Nadia.

"Oh for God's sakes, yes, yes, you are too young to ride alone. I can't let you do that! I just cannot!" The poor woman was getting more and more stressed out but was about to come up with a temporary solution. "Ok, listen to me! Sit right here and do not move! Understand?"

"Yes, ma'am, I understand."

"I will be right back. I am going to ask that nice lady in the back to watch you for a few minutes until I go back to the main car and figure out what to do next. I have the work manual there. There has to be something in it about this type of situation."

Nadia was a little confused trying to remember that she

didn't see anyone in this car. She wasn't about to question the conductor. She decided to play along and shook her head "yes." The conductor straightened out her uniform and turned to the right, heading towards Natalia, who by now was utterly baffled by the whole scene.

For the past few minutes, the freshly-awakened woman with a severe headache had been observing a bizarre situation. A conductor, whose words sounded very clear, was talking to an invisible girl that the confused Natalia couldn't hear or see. Now, that same woman was walking towards Natalia with a facial expression of someone who was on a mission.

Natalia switched the ticket into her left hand and held it up high, slightly turning her body towards the window. She wasn't going to be rude but was not in the mood to converse either. Between the conductor's bizarre behavior and her coming over to check the same ticket for the fourth time, Natalia didn't feel like being friendly.

"Excuse me, ma'am, what's your name?" the conductor asked.

"Natalia Lebedeva. Why do you ask?"

"Dear, Ms. Lebedeva, I have a huge favor to ask of you! If you don't help me, I can get in big trouble and lose my job."

"Uh! OK, go ahead, tell me what you need me to help you with." Even though Natalia was still very annoyed by the conductor, her genuinely kind nature couldn't allow her to stay mad for too long. By now she figured that the woman was either having a breakdown or was suffering from a split personality disorder.

"Oh, thank you so much, dear Natalia! Thank you! So, there is a little girl a few rows down who got on this train alone. She can't stay on it without an adult. She is only 10. Her mother is waiting for her at the central train station, but that's still two hours away!" The conductor paused, trying to read Natalia's facial expressions.

"Ok, and how can I possibly help you with that?" Natalia asked. By now, she was sure that the woman was in the midst of losing her mind.

"All I need you to do is to watch her for me, at least for 10-15 minutes. I have to go back to the main car, find the manual and figure out what to do next. I can't take her with me because all the passengers will see her and will know something is wrong. I will most likely get fired if my supervisors find out about this, so I just want to try and check the workbook. Who knows, maybe there are other options to handle this type of scenario." Her face was tense, and it looked like she was about to cry. "The girl can just sit right across from you. As long as you have your eyes on her while I am gone, I would be forever grateful to you. Please!"

At this point, Natalia was getting quite amused. She even felt like playing along with the woman. The whole scene seemed to have quite an impressive plot. The conversation Natalia was having with the conductor was the most exciting one she had in a very long time. It was a lot different from her daily world of numbers and reports.

"Ok, don't you worry, I will help you." She answered. "And, you know what? Why don't I just watch her for the whole remaining ride? I mean, I might as well. You can come and get her as soon as the train stops. What do you say to that? I bet you like that offer!" said Natalia with a smile on her face. She was trying very hard to stop her smile from turning into a full-blown laugh. She was feeling great in the role she was playing and was all into it. It felt like a soap opera.

"Are you serious? Would you do that for me? Oh my God! You are amazing! I always knew you were kind! I see you ride this train all the time! I just knew that you were beautiful on the inside and outside!"

"Thanks, for the compliment, but go get that girl before I change my mind!" Natalia sounded a little sarcastic. Evidently, the conductor didn't realize that Natalia was trying to be funny.

The moment the conductor turned around and started to walk away, Natalia covered her mouth with both of her hands and bent down. Her headache was gone, and her new problem was to try and contain the laugh that was forming. Luckily, a moment later, she got hold of her emotions and sat up, fixing her hair. She was excited and ready for the next part of this entertainment.

The conductor quickly walked up to Nadia and with a stern face bent down closer. "The nice lady at the end of this car will watch you for the rest of the ride. Do not let me find out that you weren't behaving or that you left her sight. Do you understand me?" Her eyes were frightening, and Nadia wasn't going to ask any questions or say anything back. She didn't know how to react. She was still under the impression that there wasn't anyone else in that car.

Nadia shook her head "yes" and clutched her doll. She just gave in to the conductor's wish since there wasn't much else she could do. The conductor extended her hand and pulled Nadia up.

Meanwhile, Natalia was peeking out into the aisle, observing the one-sided conversation. It was very amusing, up until little Nadia got out of her seat and turned her face toward the back of the car. The little girl looked straight at Natalia and their eyes locked.

The conductor was walking towards Natalia slowly but steadily, holding Nadia by her arm. The little girl's eyes were still dead set on Natalia. She didn't know what exactly she was feeling, but it was a mix of being afraid and mesmerized at the same time.

The completely confused Natalia was in shock. Her eyes were open wide. She had no idea what was going on and how the so-called soap opera turned into the conductor and Nadia now walking towards her.

"Here she is," said the conductor and gently helped the girl onto the seat across from Natalia. "Sit here and don't give this nice lady any trouble," she addressed the girl, waving her index finger in front of Nadia's confused face. She turned to Natalia, smiled and said, "Thank you again, so much!" Then, she sighed with relief and happily walked away.

Both Natalia and Nadia still had not broken their eye contact. With the conductor gone, silence filled the air. The only sounds anyone could hear were the wheels of the train that seemed to produce a strangely calming effect.

With every passing second, the look in Nadia's eyes was changing. It seemed like she wasn't fearful anymore and now was mesmerized by Natalia's beauty. The little girl was surprised by how much Natalia resembled her. It was almost like seeing herself in the future. On the other hand, Natalia was staring at Nadia for a different reason.

For the past ten years, all she dreamt about was finding her little girl, yet over the past few months, she had slowly started to lose her once-unshakeable faith. Now, here she was sitting in front of a girl who looked like a child who could easily be hers. Yes, Natalia understood that Nadia had her own family, parents, and life, but she also felt that the Universe had just given a sign that she shouldn't lose her faith.

There was something very compelling, but Natalia couldn't figure out what exactly that was. One thing she knew was that it kept her mind and heart locked in with the girl. The scenario they were in seemed to have happened against all the odds. The secure connection that Natalia was feeling inside at this very moment felt like a cruel tease from the universe. It was almost like a hurtful gesture that Natalia had to overcome. This turn of events was unbelievably twisted. Natalia's faith was now being tested to see if she still had a belief in miracles.

Natalia was feeling overwhelmed because over the past two years she had purposely avoided everything that had to do with children. She turned down everything from invitations to parties for her friend's children to simple holiday dinners where she knew there would be kids. Natalia was merely trying to avoid dredging up painful memories from her past. Now, here she was, alone with little Nadia in an empty car of this train, feeling that whatever was in store for her now, could be very unfair.

Suddenly Nadia broke eye contact and put her head down, staring at the floor. It was as if she had read Natalia's mind and felt unwelcome. Her face changed from mesmerized to unhappy, and her eyebrows came together in a scowl. Her tenseness was obvious. She was squeezing her doll and taking deep fast breaths, trying not to sob.

Even though Natalia hadn't been in the company of a child for over ten years, her motherly instincts had never left. She decided to break the silence and introduce herself just so the tension between them would ease up. "Hi, my name is Natalia. What's your name?"

No answer. The usually energized and brave Nadia was still quietly staring at the floor. She was not herself and felt confused, shy, scared and nervous - all at the same time. The little girl hadn't been around that many strangers. Other than running away from Daisy a few times, she lived a sheltered life, apart from the outside world. The only adults, with whom she was entirely comfortable, were those at the orphanage. On the other hand, Natalia wasn't that experienced either, even though she was a grown woman. She had something though that so many others didn't. She was patient. With that, Natalia decided to try another way to connect.

"Are you hungry?" Natalia addressed Nadia again and pulled out a plastic container from her lunch bag and took off the cover. Natalia had picked up a few things from the restaurant at the station where she boarded. "I have potato filled dumplings and stuffed grape leaves. They aren't warm, but I bet they still taste delicious."

Nadia was starving but didn't even look at the food. Nadia, staring down at the floor, reminded Natalia of the time when she was in the courtroom, feeling scared and out of place. Knowing how it feels to be uncomfortable, Natalia decided not to be pushy. She closed the container and put it away.

"Ok sweetie, let's do this. I won't bother you anymore. You tell me when you want to talk. Meanwhile, I will relax and try to nap. Hopefully, you can relax as well and enjoy the rest of the ride."

Natalia pushed back into the seat and closed her eyes. She wasn't sleeping and had no intentions to do so, but she did want to spend a few minutes meditating and calming her emotions. A feeling of peace and harmony filled up her mind. It felt good just to be there, in that space, despite how surreal this situation was.

A few minutes went by, and Natalia carefully opened one eye. She wanted to check on Nadia and also to see what time it was. The little girl was still staring at the floor, and her tense body language had not gone away just yet. Natalia closed her eye again and continued to concentrate on positive feelings. She always lived knowing that every situation had a specific lesson or reason for it. Natalia understood that there is something that can be learned even from unpleasant experiences. Even now, at that very moment, she believed that everything that was happening to her had a purpose.

As Natalia was trying to concentrate on staying at peace, a few thoughts popped into her head. Some of the things she heard earlier just didn't make sense, and nothing seemed to add up. The little girl was wet, dirty, had messy hair and was not wearing warm enough clothes. Her boots were very worn-out, and her coat was way too thin for the winter.

If what she heard the conductor say is correct, and Nadia does have both parents, then she should be in better condition. On top of all that, there was the whole part where the father apparently let her go on the train alone, and that didn't make much sense either. All that just didn't look like a logical chain of events.

Natalia had been traveling by train almost daily and for the past two years. During that whole time, she had never seen a young child or anyone under at least eighteen years of age traveling alone. Even the doll the little girl was holding made no sense. It was naked with both of the eyes completely missing out of their sockets. The doll's hair was blond but had black marks all over it, almost as if someone had colored it on purpose. It was strange that her parents would let her play with that kind of creepy looking doll. Nothing was adding up, making Natalia feel uneasy.

After another few minutes went by, Natalia decided to open her eyes and try talking to Nadia again. Just before she did that, the little girl mumbled something under her breath. "Nadia! My name is Nadia!" She didn't say it loudly, but just enough to be heard.

Natalia opened her eyes and smiled. She was looking right

at Nadia, but the grouchy girl didn't know that yet. Her eyes were still looking down, and the girl assumed that Natalia was asleep. When she didn't hear any response back, she decided to repeat herself. This time much louder.

"I SAID, my name is Nadia!" She repeated it loudly and finally looked up. Their eyes met again, but this time it felt different. Nadia didn't look scared or tense any longer. She seemed more friendly and open, almost like she had gotten over the initial barrier.

"My full name is Nadejda, but everyone calls me Nadia," she added and carefully placed her doll on the window seat next to her. "My name has a meaning, you know. The new teacher at my orphanage said that it means 'hope.'"

The second Nadia finished the sentence her eyes opened wide, and she covered her mouth with both hands. The fear showing in her eyes was overwhelming. The poor little girl instantly realized that she had just blown her cover.

"Nadia? What did you just say? What teacher? From what orphanage? You said a teacher from your orphanage!" Natalia was gasping for air, and her heart started to beat very fast. She didn't know how to react or what to do. She moved closer to Nadia's face, with only a few inches separating their eyes and asked her again.

"Please tell me, are you from an orphanage?"

"Uh-uh." Nadia made a humming sound, as her head moved from side to side.

"Nadia, please answer me. Did you lie about having a father who put you on this train and a mother who is waiting for you at the central station?"

"Uh-uh." Nadia hummed again. She was trying her best to make sure that Natalia understood that her answer was a 'no.'

"Are you LYING to me?" Natalia asked in a much more

strict way. She didn't realize that she was pushing Nadia a little too hard. She was just trying to get to the bottom of what was going on. "Are you telling me lies? Beautiful little girls like you are not supposed to lie! Please, tell me the truth." She paused.

"OK! FINE! I WAS lying!" screamed the aggravated and upset Nadia. "So what? Is there a problem if I lived in an orphanage? I am not different from other girls who live with their parents. I am still me! Now you know it all! Oh and no one is waiting for me anywhere, just like no one put me on this train! I lied about that too. I said that to the conductor so I could get on! I just ran away!" Nadia had a hidden temper, but it only came out if someone pushed or pressured her too hard.

Natalia was numb. From what she just heard, this little girl could be her lost daughter. The poor woman's hopes were rising by the second. She had no idea that those same dreams were about to be shattered by what Nadia was about to say next.

CHAPTER NINE

I t seemed like the little girl was full of anger and hate. That wasn't the case. She was just desperate for love and didn't know how to express it other than with rage and hurtfulness. "Oh, guess what? Even though I do have parents, I have never seen them in my life! I only know that they were bad alcoholics and gave me to the orphanage as soon as I was born but that's all I know about them! Happy? Now you know all the truth, so there! Now leave me alone!" Nadia's eyes were full of tears. She didn't want to say anything about her past life; but, under pressure from Natalia, she had no choice but, to be honest.

Natalia was stunned and hurt at the same time. Only a minute ago, the little bright light of hope that Nadia could be hers had just disappeared into the darkness. On top of being heartbroken and disappointed Natalia felt terrible that she let herself push Nadia to this point. The strong unexplained bond and feeling that Natalia was developing towards Nadia made her emotions take over.

Natalia knew that she had no right to pressure the little girl this hard, especially since they had just met. However, it already happened, and everything was now out. Natalia asked for the truth and now wished she hadn't. The confirmation that Nadia did have both of her parents shattered Natalia's heart in half.

At the same time, Nadia's big blue eyes filling up with tears were piercing right through Natalia's soul. The poor little girl was looking at her with hope and a silent scream for help. Natalia didn't know what part of it all was the most hurtful, but the feeling was somehow familiar to her. It felt just like that terrible day when she held her little girl for the first and the last time.

Natalia extended her hands towards Nadia. She did it naturally, without second-guessing herself. Somehow Natalia knew what this child needed at that very moment; the same exact thing that Natalia was craving as well. It was love, support and a feeling of being safe, that was coming from someone she had just met.

"Come here, sweetheart, hug me. It's all going to be ok," said Natalia and gently pressed the little girl against herself.

Nadia didn't fight it. She felt safe in Natalia's arms. She couldn't even recall the last time anyone had hugged her. Now, it felt so pleasant and calming. Nadia was sensing the genuine love that was coming from Natalia, a stranger who crossed her path on this very train in this exact car.

"Sweetie, your secrets are safe with me! I promise you that!" said Natalia, still holding the little girl in her arms. Natalia knew very well that playing along with Nadia's lie to the conductor wasn't an ok thing to do, but for some strange reason, it felt right within her heart.

After a minute had gone by, Natalia gently pulled Nadia away and extended her right-hand pinky. It was a sign used by almost every child in the country to seal the friendship forever. "Are we friends for life"? Natalia asked.

"Yes, yes, yes, a friend for life!" yelled the happy Nadia and wrapped her little pinky around Natalia's finger. It was undoubtedly an adorable way to start a new friendship: the one between a runaway orphan and a lonesome woman.

"Wait. Wait for a second," said Nadia, quickly pulling her pinky back. Her face turned from happy to sad as she looked straight at Natalia. "We can only be friends until the train arrives. Then what? I thought that we made the pinky promise! So we aren't going to keep it?" She looked disappointed.

"Hmmm, well that is true, but what if we can change that?" answered Natalia and smiled. That caught Nadia's interest. She opened her eyes wider and raised her eyebrows.

"You said we could change it? How?"

"How? Well, I can make you a deal!"

"Deal? What does that mean? I never made a 'deal' before."

"If you can promise me that you will behave and do well in school, I can try and see if you can come and live with me."

"What do you mean live with you? You mean every day and every night?"

"Yes, every day and every night, and every week, and every month, and every year, until you get tired of it!"

"Is this a joke?"

"Nope, I'm not joking, as long as you are a good girl!"

"Oh My God, I can't believe it! It's like a real adoption?"

"Yup, I will have to find the way to adopt you legally, and you can live with me in my condo. I own a nice apartment in the center of Moscow in one of the new skyscrapers right by the river. It's big, and you will have your room and bathroom."

"Wait. So will we be able to go to the park and the zoo?"

"Yes! I've never been to the zoo, so, definitely yes!"

"And we will get all brand new clothes with tags?"

"Yup, brand new with tags!"

"And you will be my mommy, forever and ever?"

"Yes, and you will be my daughter, forever and ever, too!"

They both paused and looked at each other. Nadia's eyes and mouth were wide open. She wasn't as much emotional as she was shocked. "DEAL! DEAL! DEAL!" she suddenly yelled and clapped her hands, jumping up and down in her seat. "It's a deal!"

They both started to laugh and hugged each other again, but now with happiness and pure relief. Natalia's eyes were watery, but she was not going to allow herself to cry, at least not at that moment. She felt way too blessed and alive to let her tears out.

It was hard for her to comprehend what had just happened. This little girl, who looked so much like her little Nadia, just showed up out of nowhere. She got on that train. She came to that car. She was brought right to that seat, and now, here they were together, planning their future.

"Nadia, I have to tell you something that you might not even believe," said Natalia with an intriguing voice. "This train was not my original train. I was supposed to get on one that left earlier this afternoon, but I still had to finish my work, and I ended up getting a ticket to the last train--the one we are on now. Believe it or not, I have never missed a train in my life, not until this very day. It scares me to think that if I had made it onto that earlier train, I would never have met you." Natalia's face seemed almost pale just from the thought of that possibility. Meanwhile, Nadia didn't seem to be that impressed by all that.

"Well, guess what, I have something similar to tell you!" The little girl was excited. She was about to tell her something that she thought was an even better story then Natalia's. "I didn't miss any trains; but just so you know, out of the few times I tried to run away, this was the first time I made it this far. I never even saw a real train until today, so I guess your story and mine, it was all meant to be!" She was smiling with a hint of harmless sarcasm. "So, can I call you mommy from now on?"

"Yes, sweetie, you may," answered Natalia but felt that her emotions were about to get the best of her. It was getting more difficult to control the tears, but somehow she still held them in. Natalia didn't want to ruin the magical moment.

"Mommy, can Babaika come with us, too?"

"Who is Babaika?"

"It's the name I gave my doll. Just like my name, hers also stands for something. Babaika means something scary or hideous. I found her outside when I tried to run away for the first time. She was naked, and both of her eyes were missing. When I brought her inside the orphanage, all the other kids started to laugh and scream "Babaika." That's why I decided to name her like that."

"It's Ok, but why is Babaika's hair colored with a black marker?"

"Well, that's my fault. I did that because when some of the kids saw her up close, they said she is a bad girl because her hair is blond. Some others girls at Daisy said that because she was bad, her original owner poked out her eyes and threw her away. I didn't want them to think that blond girls like her and like me are bad, so I colored her hair black. After that, no one said anything nasty about her, so I was happy. One day when I'm grown up, I will color my hair dark as well."

"Nadia, please, don't even think that way about yourself. You are a brilliant girl, and Babaika is very lucky to be your doll and no one else's. Plus, blond girls aren't bad. How someone is as a person has nothing to do with hair color. Those girls are just jealous of beautiful hair that you, me, and Babaika have. That's why they said hurtful things to you."

"Oh ok, I didn't think of that. You are right! So, does that mean that my beautiful Babaika comes with us? She hasn't been out of my sight since the day I found her."

"Yes, sweetie, you can bring Babaika, too!"

They smiled at each other and Nadia got up to move to the seat between the window and Natalia. She felt a close connection with her new mother. Both of them got into their roles as mother and daughter without difficulties.

For the remaining hour, the newly formed family talked about Moscow and all the places they were going to visit together when the adoption process was final. For the first time in their lives, they were genuinely excited about New Year's Eve and Christmas. Neither one of them had ever had a real Christmas tree. Together, they quickly decided to get the biggest tree they could find and one that would fit into Natalia's apartment. They were dreaming like they were best friends. They were making the best out of their relationship, which seemed to be growing stronger by the minute.

After they made fun plans for the near future, the next item on their agenda was how they were going to get off the train when it stopped. The first option was to exit as soon as the train arrived and before the conductor got to their car. The second choice was to walk off the train with the conductor but then quickly hide among the busy crowd and go to the local police. In both cases, Natalia was going to end up doing all that she had to do legally for a smooth adoption. The last thing she needed is for someone to reverse the process due to incorrect or illegal activities. She wasn't going to let that happen.

Natalia decided to give her statement to the local police department right near her house. She planned to tell them that she found Nadia at the original location where she had boarded the train. Natalia wasn't going to mention anything about Pavlovo. Nadia herself was going to say that she doesn't know her address, last name or where her parents are. She was planning on telling the court that she had lived a very sheltered life and homeschooled. With all that planned out, Natalia hoped that there wouldn't be any issues about adopting the so-called neglected and lost girl.

Natalia felt right about going to the police station this time around. It was going to be much different from the time she went to the police ten years ago. The new Natalia was an intelligent woman with very high education and a prestigious job. She was dressed in the most current fashion and drove a Mercedes Benz 500, just because she loved the way it looked. The average cops were making a tenth of her yearly salary and wouldn't even question the truthfulness of her statements.

After the girls finalized both of their plans, Natalia decided to write a little note for the conductor. She wanted to leave her a thank you message, just in case, they were able to get out of the car before she got there. Natalia grabbed a pen from her purse. She wrote down her contact information on one side of a small piece of paper and a few lines on the other side. When she finished, she folded it in half and held it carefully in her hand until the train arrived at the station.

The conductor wasn't in their sight and the time had come for the young family to make their move. Natalia placed the note on the seat, and they quickly walked out. The second they got outside, they broke down with laughter, like two best friends who had just done something wrong together. It was a very heartwarming sight, but they didn't realize how close they still were to the train.

It only took a few more seconds for the conductor to walk into the last car. Of course, the woman didn't see Nadia or Natalia there, but did find the folded note on the seat and grabbed it quickly. On the outside of it, she saw written information that Natalia wanted her to have. There were things like Natalia's address, landline and cell phone numbers, her work address, and even her driver's license number. She scanned the info and opened up the note.

Hello, dear angel. After Nadia and I spent the past two hours together, we realized how many things we have in common. I also found out that her family has abandoned her and I can't let her be homeless, especially in a big city like Moscow. With that said, upon our arrival at the station, I intend to go to the police and to file a report. I will tell them that I saw her alone at the train station where I initially boarded, and after talking to her, I found out that she had nowhere to go. I'm going to report that I had purchased her train ticket because I didn't want to leave her at that station alone. I will also tell them that I am willing to take her on and am going to do all the proper and legal paperwork for the adoption. I can assure you that I will not mention your name to anyone, now or later.

P.S. Thank you for being our angel and for giving us the hope and love we both desire so much.

The conductor pressed the note into her chest pocket and tears started to roll down her face. Then she heard distinct laughter and looked up, peering through the window. The station was full of people, but she was still able to see Natalia and Nadia not more than fifteen feet away from the train. They were laughing and holding hands, slowly disappearing into the bustling crowd.

The conductor knew that she had played a most significant role in their lives that very day. After all those twenty years of working on different trains and thinking that her job wasn't notable, she changed her mind. She was happy that she ended up being a connecting link between two people who desperately needed each other. She was now sure that God had placed her in the right place, at the right time and for the right reason. She was indeed an angel.

. . .

For the new family, the adoption process and all the legal requirements were going very smoothly. It was going to take only a couple of weeks. The courts could not find any information about the little girl in any of their records. The only things they knew were what Natalia had written in the police report and what they had heard from Nadia during the interview.

Nadia didn't give them much information and told them just a few things. She said that she only knew her parent's first names and her birthday, which was May 2nd. She told the judge that she didn't even know her address and that her alcoholic parents didn't care if she went to school or stayed home. Overall, Nadia's story was very creative and hard to believe, but it worked.

The court system had no choice but to award Natalia full

custody of Nadia, due to the inability to establish her identity. The only requirement that the judge put in place was that the social workers from child services would have to visit Natalia's condo every six months. The court wanted to makes sure that Nadia was safe and well adjusted. That didn't make the new family worried much.

Meanwhile, the director of the Daisy orphanage filled out a missing child report with the local police and contacted the department of child safety. Those types of cases usually took several months for the investigations even to begin. The system was full of reports of kidnappings and runaways. No one was going to look for little Nadia anytime soon. Her old life was over, and an exciting new one had just begun.

Nadia was amazed at everything she saw, from the moment they got off the train. The enormous amount of people she saw at the station was overwhelming, but she was doing well at keeping herself calm. When they made it to the long-term parking lot where Natalia left her car, Nadia got a partial glimpse of her new lifestyle.

Natalia had good taste when it came to beautiful things. Her latest purchase was a brand new two-door Mercedes Benz 500. The outside color of the car was dark blue, but an added coat of shimmer made the whole vehicle shine under any light. The inside of the vehicle was beige leather with dark blue stitching to match the exterior.

Nadia was eager to see the interior of the car. When she got in and sat down, she started to clap her hands. Her seat was so low that it felt like she was sitting down on the ground. Also the moment Natalia turned on the engine of her car, its whole interior filled up with beautiful blue neon lights.

Nadia was mesmerized. The eye-catching screen of the GPS in the middle of the dashboard and the sound of the woman asking Natalia for directions made it hard for Nadia to look away. At the same time, the little strawberry-shaped air fresheners inside of the vents were giving out the yummy aroma of fresh fruits.

When Natalia got onto the main road, Nadia shifted her attention and started to look through the window. She couldn't believe the unlimited amount of cars and street lights they were passing. Another ten minutes later, Natalia took a side street and slowed down. She didn't live that far from the train station, and a few minutes later they got to her building.

As Natalia pulled up to the gate of the underground parking garage and pressed the button, Nadia rolled down her window. She wanted to check out the height of the building up close. It was so high that the top floor was not even visible. It seemed to dissolve somewhere in the dark Moscow sky, beautifully covered with millions of bright stars.

Natalia smiled and pressed the button to get into the garage. It was for the residents and visitors with passes. After she parked, they got out and headed toward the elevator. When they arrived, Natalia pressed the button for the 15th floor. As soon as the elevator started to go up, Nadia grabbed onto Natalia's hand. She had never ridden on one before, and the speed with which they were going up, made her stomach feel funny.

When they got to the condo and Natalia unlocked the door, Nadia didn't rush in. She was nervous and still a bit shy. For her, it was only the second place she had ever lived.

Natalia opened the door all the way and gently pushed Nadia forward. It wasn't the easiest of the moments for her either. She had never had a child cross the doorway of her apartment, never mind a 10-year-old girl whose name was Nadia. It was hard for Natalia just like it was scary for Nadia, but it was all for the better.

"We are finally home!" she said to Nadia and started to take off her high-heeled shoes.

"Wow! Your home is beautiful!" answered Nadia, slowly taking a few steps and looking around at the walls and the furniture.

"Our home," corrected Natalia. "This is now our home."

Natalia smiled and carefully placed her shoes on the floor.

"Let me show you around. Let's start with the kitchen."

Nadia shook her head "yes" and quickly took off her boots. She walked over to Natalia and got in front of her. Everything she looked at was beautiful. The floors, the furniture, and even the high ceiling, with its shiny crystal chandelier, were luxurious and modern. It was evident that whoever designed that apartment indeed had a perfect eye for beauty.

The kitchen was very spacious and had an island with a blue and gold granite countertop. The cabinets were a mix of grey and a dark bluish color with shiny, gold-finished handles. The chairs behind the kitchen island were tall and had soft leather cushions. The floor throughout the whole condo was white marble. It had sporadic shimmery gold lines giving it a chic, yet exotic look.

Natalia's condo had three large bedrooms and two and a half baths. The master bedroom had a high king size bed with triple steps next to it, for easy access. The bedroom also had a balcony with sliding glass doors. Out of all the rooms in the house, it had the best view of the city. As long as Nadia was not afraid of heights, she was going to see Moscow in its compelling beauty. The Moscow River, buildings, and even the Red Square were all visible right from that balcony. Even the beautiful night sky could be observed, not only from the balcony but also from the bed itself.

The other two bedrooms were on the other side of the condo. Those windows overlooked the outer side of the city, away from the center and bright lights. Natalia's apartment was in the most desirable location of the building. Not only was it a corner unit with multiple views, but it was also the closest to the elevators.

To Nadia's surprise, the master bedroom was not used. It had everything nicely set, but no signs of Natalia sleeping there.

"Mom, isn't this bedroom the biggest one?"

"Yes, sweetie it is."

"So, then why does it look empty? Aren't you sleeping here?"

"No, I sleep in the smaller bedroom on the other side."

"Oh? I'm surprised. I thought you would want to see the city and its bright lights at night."

Natalia's face looked pale. She didn't want to talk about the night city or why she wanted nothing to do with it. "Honey, I don't like bright lights. This bedroom was waiting for you!"

"Oh my God, mommy, thank you! It's mine! It's mine!"

Nadia was so happy that she didn't even read anything into her mother's answer. On the other hand, Natalia did her best not to show Nadia the true feelings she had towards Moscow at night.

"Mommy, I have never even had a bed to myself let alone my bedroom!"

"I understand. I didn't either, not until I got this condo." Natalia replied.

All of a sudden, Nadia ran towards the back of the bedroom where she saw the door into the master bathroom. When she ran in there, she started to scream with joy. The bathroom was just as big as the bedroom itself. It was so easy to make Nadia happy.

"Mommy, this bathroom is huge. Oh my God! Is this the best bathroom you have ever seen or what?" Nadia was beside herself.

"Sweetie, let's clean up and eat. I am starving. I'll bet you are hungry as well. I will give you some of my clothes for now; but, in the morning we are going to get you all brand new stuff. Plus, you will need a few things for your school." She said and walked away.

Natalia was emotional. Having a little girl in her home was a big responsibility. It made her scared and excited, all at the same time. Natalia worried that one day the truth about her past was going to come out and Nadia was not going to be able to understand. She didn't want to lose the one person whose opinion she cared about and to whom she was now attached.

The next morning Natalia took Nadia to the shopping center. It was still early and the roads, as well as the mall, weren't as busy yet. Natalia decided not to take the car because on the way back they would be stuck in the lunch-time rush hour. It would have made it much longer to drive back home than to walk. Plus, it was not that far from her condo anyway.

They got to the mall without any trouble, although people were already starting to accumulate and the traffic was starting to get congested. Unfortunately, after they finished, it was already two-thirty in the afternoon. By that time it seemed like the whole city was out and about.

Moscow is the largest city in the country and has over 11 million residents living there. Also, there are over 15 million visitors from all around the world every single year. The most common area for the tourists and the citizens was usually the central part of the city. The mall, especially on the weekends was always packed.

When Natalia and Nadia finally went onto the main street and started to walk, there were loads of people, cars, bicycles and regular traffic. The loud noises coming from every source were overwhelming to both of them. Nadia was always known to be a brave, but even for her, all of these at once was too much. She was holding on to Natalia's hand with a death grip. They kept up a rapid and steady pace so that they could get home fast.

When they finally made it to the building, Nadia grabbed the shopping bags from Natalia's hands and headed towards the elevator. She just wanted to be helpful. It looked like they had a powerful yet silent connection and knew each other's thoughts and feelings without using any words.

They spent that evening at home, making dinner and relaxing. At the end of the night, Natalia got onto her laptop to check a few essential work emails. Meanwhile, Nadia went into her room and started to put away her new clothes. She also picked out the outfit that she was going to wear to school on Monday. So far, Nadia was happy and excited about her new life.

That night the brave little girl slept by herself in the big bedroom. The bed was so high that while lying on it, Nadia could easily see the city through the glass doors of the balcony. She always wanted to see Moscow, especially at night. It was her lifelong dream to visit the Red Square, the Kremlin and to see the famous clock. I guess, when you dream about something all of the time, sooner or later those thoughts become a reality.

On Monday morning, Natalia prepared Nadia's lunch, braided her hair in two beautiful braids and took her to the new school. It wasn't far from the building, but it took at least twenty-five minutes due to the morning rush hour. Nadia wasn't nervous but was undoubtedly curious. She hadn't seen a real school or an actual classroom ever before.

When they got there, Nadia was a little surprised. It was an all-girls school. She didn't realize that Natalia decided not to sign her up for a regular one. She had no idea how Natalia felt about men and even boys, including boys of Nadia's age. Natalia didn't want her daughter to be around any males at all, at least for now. The all-girls school was the most expensive to attend out of the whole city but also the safest one. Nadia didn't seem to care where she attended school. She just wanted to meet new friends and have fun.

The principal ended up being a lovely lady. The staff was as well. They made Natalia and Nadia feel very welcome. No one asked any personal questions. The school had one goal - getting an education and following the school's rules. Those two things were their most significant priorities. The testing Nadia had to go through was quick. It only took a little over an hour to complete the test of her IQ and the knowledge of a few core subjects.

When the testing was over Nadia came out and sat down next to Natalia to wait for the results. They didn't talk much, and fifteen minutes later one of the teachers came out, calling them into the principal's office. Both Natalia and Nadia looked at each other in a surprised manner. They didn't know if the fast results were a good or a bad thing. They walked in and sat down.

"Good morning, ladies," said the principal with a smile. She looked quite happy.

"Good Morning Mrs. . ?" asked Natalia, with a question mark.

"Mrs. Zolotova. My apologies for not introducing myself."

"Good morning, Mrs. Zolotova. I'm Natalia Lebedeva, and Nadia is my daughter."

"It is very nice to meet you, Ms. Lebedeva and your beautiful daughter, Nadia, as well. We are pleased to have you here and hope that you will choose to attend our school."

"Well, yes, of course, we would love that, but we weren't sure if you have accepted her already or not. Did she pass all the tests?"

"Did she pass everything? It will be our HONOR to have her here! She tested at least three grades ahead of her age on every core subject, and her IQ score came back as 130. We have never had any girls of her age or even older than that scoring this high. We don't even know if she would be interested in our curriculum, but we are hoping that you will give us a chance to create special material just for her to make it interesting."

"Wow. 130 IQ? That's very impressive. It's almost as high as mine. I'm sure she will be happy to stay here. Is that right, sweetie?" Natalia turned and looked at Nadia.

"Yes, mom, I would like to stay in this school, please."

"That's great! Welcome to your new home, Nadia!" said the principle with excitement as she looked at the proud new student. "Also, Ms. Lebedeva, as a principal I have to let you know, that Nadia is fully eligible to be placed in the eighth grade with 13-year-old girls. It's totally up to you."

"Thank you! I am sure she would love to skip a few years of school, but I would leave that decision for Nadia to make."

"Uhh, mom, can I just stay in the grade with all the other 10-year-old girls? Grade eight and nine are cool but the girls are much older, and I might not have as many friends. Please?"

"Ok, sweetheart, no worries. It's completely up to you. We can revisit this idea in the future."

Nadia smiled back at Natalia, and they exchanged a silent, yet mutual understanding. The director finished all the required paperwork and took Nadia into the classroom. Natalia thanked everyone and left the school. She had a busy day ahead of her and needed to catch up on things at work.

Even though from that day and on she had a new daily schedule, she didn't mind her new routine. She was able to work from 8 a.m. to 3 p.m. and finish the rest from home in the evening. Nadia usually did her homework then, too.

A few days into that week, Natalia asked her boss to switch her work schedule, so she wouldn't have to travel more than a few hours each day. She wanted to make sure that she was able to bring Nadia to school and pick her up as well. Her boss had no issues with that. He was very well aware that Natalia had worked double and sometimes triple the number of hours each week, during the past two years.

The new lifestyle Natalia now had improved her quality of life and the level of her happiness dramatically. She loved her new role as a mom and was terrific at it. Nadia also was doing great in school and at home. They got along very well, and their friendship was solid.

When the school year was coming to an end, Nadia decided to continue staying at the same grade level as her friends. She realized that she was smarter than most of the kids there, but spending time with her friends every day was much more essential. Natalia was okay with that. Nadia's happiness became her main priority.

As Nadia's 11th birthday was approaching, she decided to ask Natalia if she could have her first-ever birthday party. Nadia found the perfect timing to talk to her mother. She grabbed her third-quarter report card with all A's and came up to Natalia.

"Mom, is it ok if I invite a few of my friends for my 11th birthday? I know this birthday is not a big number, but I never had a birthday celebration. It will be my first one," said Nadia and handed the grade card to Natalia.

"Um. Yes. Sure, go ahead. It's fine with me. Just tell me on which day," answered Natalia and smiled. She only glanced over the report card for a split second. She already knew what was in it. "If the birthday lands on a weekday, people usually celebrate it on that same weekend. Would that be alright?"

"Yes sure, let's do it on Saturday, May 5th. That's only three days after my actual birthday. Is that ok?"

"Yes, I guess its ok. We can do that."

"Yay! Thank you, mommy. I will go make the guest list now!"

Nadia ran to her room to write down the names of all the girls she wanted to invite, while Natalia stood there in a fog. She remembered that Nadia told her after they got off the train that her birthday was May 2nd, but it didn't hit her until this very moment. Nadia's birthday was the same date and year as her little girl's. Fate couldn't have been any crueler than this. From now on, the poor woman would have to celebrate Nadia's birthday on the same exact day as she would have for her daughter.

Natalia had no choice. She couldn't justify punishing Nadia for what happened eleven years ago. Indeed, it was not Nadia's fault that she was born on that exact day. It was now up to Natalia to find a way to deal with her loss without affecting her new life. With a heavy heart, she ended up holding a big birthday party at their apartment. There was a lot of food, music, games, and fun.

Nadia was able to invite twenty girls from her school, and even Natalia decided to ask a few of her co-workers who had daughters to join them. They named the birthday party "all-girls fun night," and the title matched it perfectly. That day was ironically the first time any of Natalia's friends or co-workers had visited her home. It was better later than never.

There is no denying that Natalia was emotional the whole night, but she didn't show it to anyone. It was all about her new daughter. It was all about Nadia. Somehow, Natalia had shifted her mind and priorities in the right direction. It was her new life, and she had to leave the past in the sacred spot deep in her heart. It was time to finally be happy and to move on.

CHAPTER TEN

As time went on, and Nadia was becoming a teenager, her personality started to change. She was getting more comfortable with her new home and the lifestyle but was also beginning to get curious about things. Nadia started to notice small details from her everyday life that she hadn't paid any attention to up until now. Unfortunately, most of those had something to do with the past, not only hers but also Natalia's. She started to question and wanted to get the answers.

One day a few weeks before New Year's Eve, Nadia finally decided to talk to her mother. She wanted to tell her what's been bothering her lately and was hoping that their conversation was going to get her some clarity. Nadia finished her homework and walked into the kitchen. Natalia was making a salad and working on their dinner.

"Mom, I need to talk to you about a couple of things that have been on my mind for quite some time now."

"Ok. Nadia, I'm listening," answered Natalia with curiosity.

"Well, I have been living here for the past three years and my fourteenth birthday is coming up a few months from now. I think I am old enough now to learn about my origin and where exactly I was I born. I also have a few questions about your past life."

Natalia's eyes opened wide, and she squeezed the handle of the cutting knife she was using. It was hard for her to control her emotions. Nadia caught her off guard and was now standing right there watching Natalia's body language and facial expressions. The now curious Nadia continued, "Not only have we never talked about my life up until the day I met you, but we haven't discussed your childhood either. I don't even know where your parents are or any of your relatives for that matter. I have many unanswered questions, and they are bothering me more and more every day. I want to know who my birth parents are and why they decided to give me up to the orphanage. I want to find out if I might have brothers and sisters, or other relatives, somewhere out there. I want to finally confront my biological mother and ask her how she could give me away and never come back to get me."

Nadia was looking at Natalia with a hunger for answers. It was a good thing that she trusted her mother enough to open up to her. It's not like Nadia's questions were unfair or outrageous. They were regular things that any human being would want to know.

In some strange ways, Nadia's questions made Natalia think about her parents as well. Undoubtedly, it was possible that one day she also would want to confront them. She wanted to ask how they could sell her to the sex-trafficking organization, never mind for ten bottles of vodka. Those cold facts were unchangeable and mind-blowing. That's why Natalia had learned so well to suppress her memory. On the other hand, it was clear that Nadia wasn't interested in doing the same.

"Mom, I also want to know why you don't have any very close friends. Why haven't I seen you go on a date? You are only thirty years old, yet you don't have a boyfriend or seem to be interested in finding one. The only guy I ever hear you talk to is your boss. I mean, don't you want to have a boyfriend, a husband or even children?"

Natalia was getting more and more anxious. She was not ready to face any of these questions nor was she prepared to tell Nadia the details about her past. She didn't want Nadia to know all the horrible things she did when she was almost her age. Natalia just stood there, not knowing what to say. Unfortunately, Nadia wasn't going to back away and still stood there, waiting for answers.

"Nadia, I understand your concerns, and if I were you, I would probably be just as curious. The thing is that there isn't much for me to say. I honestly have no idea who your biological parents are or where they live. I surely have no idea why they brought you to the orphanage, but there is one thing that I know for sure right now. I know that it's much better to concentrate on the present and the future. Why would you want to dig into the past and bring back things that you might not like?" answered Natalia hurriedly, hoping that would satisfy Nadia's questions. It didn't--not even close.

"Mom, I don't even care to find out the information about my parents as much as I would like to know about your past. You are my only parent now, yet I feel like I don't know you. I just want to learn things about you and your family. I want to know where you were born, who your parents were, and which colleges you have attended. Are those questions too much to ask?" It was apparent, Nadia was getting very annoyed. She didn't understand Natalia's reaction and felt that she was secretive.

Not knowing how to get out of that conversation without being rude or ignorant, Natalia came up with a better excuse. "Sweetie, I'm exhausted and still have to make the dinner. Why don't we talk about this some other time like maybe after the holidays?"

Nadia, seeing that it wasn't going to be as easy of a conversation as she was hoping for, decided to continue it at another time.

"Ok mom, if you are tired, we can talk about it some other time, perhaps in a few weeks?"

That's just what Natalia wanted to hear. "Ok sweetie, perfect. We can chat at that time. I appreciate your understanding." She was relieved but felt uneasy about it. "I'm going to go to my room and lie down for a few minutes. Please feel free to eat whatever you want from the fridge, or you can finish making the salad and eat without me." Natalia put down what she was doing and exited the kitchen

She stayed in her room for the rest of the night. It was the first time in years that Natalia had cried herself to sleep. The poor woman knew that now it's just a matter of time before Nadia finds out all the secrets that Natalia has been hiding. Nadia was just too smart not to figure things out. Lying to her made no sense.

After that night, Nadia had not brought up their conversation for the next few weeks. Natalia started to forget about Nadia's questions and was busy every day and night with her work and her daughter's activities. Nadia took piano and ballet lessons, played tennis and attended painting classes. To top it all off Natalia's work schedule was full as well. It was the end of the year, which was always the busiest time for the company. She had to submit dozens of financial reports and completed audits to the Moscow tax department. She had her hands full.

Meanwhile, Nadia was also busy with all of her exams and activities. She had dozens of friends, and between them and her extra-curricular activities, she hadn't approached Natalia with the questions again. For the time being, Nadia seemed content.

Natalia knew that sooner or later she would have to tell her daughter the truth, but she wasn't going to be the one to bring that up. If it were up to Natalia, she would take all of her secrets into the next life. Unfortunately, that was highly unlikely. Thankfully, for now, the holidays were the only thing that was occupying everyone's mind. January was approaching fast, and so was the day to open up about her past life.

The New Year's Eve celebration was the most significant holiday for anyone living in Russia. The traditions were pretty similar for most of the families. All day long food was being cooked, and old movies would play on TV. These were the same exact movies as every prior year and for the past couple of decades. Towards the late evening is when those who celebrated it at home started to prepare the dinner table. The guests would arrive between 9 and 10 o'clock at night, and the TV would get set on the primary station, which was channel number 1. For the next couple of hours, all the famous singers would give New Year's Eve performances, and that's when everyone would be eating.

At precisely 11:55 p.m. the president of Russia would go on live TV and address the nation. He would talk about the year that was about to end and what achievements the country had made. Then he would wish good luck to everyone in the upcoming New Year. After that when the time hit 12 a.m., the big clock in the Red Square would chime, and twelve loud sounds would indicate that the New Year had started.

The person at the head of the table would pop open a bottle of champagne and people would toast each other. Then, everyone would watch the fantastic fireworks from the windows of their homes. Most of the people would leave after the desserts and would visit other friends and families, hopping from house to house. That went on until the early morning hours. The tradition was fun and always memorable.

After Natalia got out of jail, she had spent every New Year's Eve at home. When Nadia moved in, they also stayed home, but at least now they celebrated it together. For some reason, Natalia felt that Nadia wanted more. Maybe because she kept mentioning about different house parties that her friends were going to have and how much fun it would be to celebrate it with lots of people. Natalia decided to surprise her daughter and celebrate the New Year's Eve with all of her co-workers and their families. Her boss held a yearly party for all of his employees and their close family members. He always chose excellent locations for it and this year the celebration was at a restaurant on the top floor of a skyscraper hotel in the center of the city.

When Natalia told Nadia about the new plan, the girl was beyond excited. Natalia rarely took Nadia out, never mind to a party. She was just a little overprotective when it came to Nadia, not that it was a bad thing to be, especially of a beautiful 13-year-old girl.

Nadia, on the other hand, didn't feel that she needed any guarding by her mother. She was brave and by now had opened up and was becoming a social butterfly. Nadia thought that it was the right age to experience new things, to meet other kids and to build life-long friendships. Natalia saw herself in Nadia, at least up until she was 14. It's shocking, how much one event can change a child, making an outgoing and loving girl into a mostly sad and introverted woman.

Despite being a little nervous about her choice for New Year's Eve, Natalia was a bit excited as well. Having Nadia there for the past few years had made her more comfortable with other people. She was more relaxed, less worried about others and more talkative and social. On several occasions, Nadia saw her talking to other parents at the school meetings and other events. That was considered a significant achievement.

When December 31st came around, Natalia explained to Nadia that there would be lots of people at the party and many of them will have their sons there as well. Natalia wanted to make sure that her daughter knew not to get friendly with any boys and to stay in her sight for the duration of the night. Nadia found that amusing and assured Natalia that she had no plans for socializing or meeting any boys. That was not even on her mind. She was more concerned with which dress she would wear.

That evening, they got dressed and ready in their bedrooms. When they both finally came out and saw each other, they started to laugh. The two of them, standing and facing each other looked like they were twins, only one was taller than the other. Their body shape, hair, makeup, and even posture, looked almost identical. Natalia couldn't believe how much older Nadia looked when all dolled up. She was growing and maturing. Her fourteenth birthday was only a few months away. Natalia had to learn to deal with it. That was the fate of every parent in the world.

When they got to the party, they instantly became the center of attention. They looked like fashion models: tall, skinny, blond, and ideally put together. All the men and even women at the party were staring at them. Other than people who worked with Natalia, no one could tell that they were a mother and daughter. Being all dressed up, Nadia looked much older than her age, and Natalia looked much younger than hers. They looked like sisters.

A few of Natalia's closest co-workers quickly came up to introduce their family members. Natalia felt uncomfortable with all the eyes on her, but Nadia felt great. The girl loved the attention and social events. She wasn't shy anymore.

While Natalia was busy socializing, some of the men she worked with already had their eyes on her. Most of them were from the upper management and saw the party as a perfect opportunity to approach Natalia. There were no other work events that she had attended in the past, only the meetings. It was quite humorous to see the way guys were coming up to her one after another, throughout the evening.

Since Natalia had started to work at her company almost five years back, no one had ever seen her with a guy or heard of her going on any dates. She seemed not to be interested in any of the guys. At one point, about a year ago, someone started the gossip that Natalia might be into women. That chatter went away very quickly after she almost got into a fight when a gay secretary inappropriately touched her in the cafeteria.

As soon as the president wished everyone a happy 2004, the music went back on, and the fun part of the party started. Natalia became even more annoyed because now she was getting asked to dance by different guys every few minutes. She wanted to leave, but Nadia had a blast dancing with her new friends. The next time Nadia looked back, Natalia signaled her to come to the table.

Even though Nadia was having fun and wanted to stay longer,

she understood that Natalia was tired and it was very late. They decided to go and said goodbye to those people they knew and those they had just met. Nadia thought it was funny how the two of them were the first people to leave, but she didn't care. That was because Nadia already had something else in mind. The minute they got into the elevator it was time for Nadia to ask for the favor.

"Mom, can we please take a ride throughout the downtown and check out the city? I never saw Moscow at night! Please!"

"What? No. I'm sorry. I'm too tired, and I don't want to drive around the city, especially in the snow!"

"Mom, please! I want to see the big Christmas tree and the Red Square with the clock tower we just saw on TV. That would be so awesome! Please, just for a few minutes."

"I said no!"

"Mom, don't say no. I don't usually ask you for much. It's just such a special night of celebration, and we are already out. I would love to add more amazing memories to an already magical night!" Nadia continued begging. She was determined, but Natalia was still not convinced.

They got out of the elevator on the basement floor and walked over to the car. Natalia was still not saying anything back. Nadia decided to try a different approach.

"Mom, it's ok if you don't want to go there. I will ask my friend, Alice, later on, today. Her father will take her and me to check out the Christmas tree at night. He doesn't mind so you don't have to." Nadia hoped that by saying that, Natalia might agree. She always made it very obvious that she wanted Nadia not to be near any men of any age.

"Are you trying to blackmail me?" replied Natalia.

"No mom, not at all," said Nadia with sarcasm and a smirk.

"Fine," snapped Natalia. Then she paused. "We'll go!"

Nadia couldn't control her reaction, "Yay, yay, yay, thank you, mommy!" She hugged Natalia and put on her seatbelt.

The moment Natalia drove out of the parking garage, sizeable, fluffy snowflakes started to land on her windshield. The snow wasn't the biggest issue. Instead, it was the slippery road. The visibility wasn't good at all. It was a bad idea to drive around in that weather, but Natalia felt that she had to do it. The last thing she wanted was for Nadia to come back to the city with Alice and her dad.

Natalia drove slowly and kept the speed at around 10 miles per hour. A couple of minutes into driving they entered the main street that leads towards the center. Natalia slowed down and dropped her speed in half. She was concentrating on the road that somehow looked very familiar. Surely, even if she worked in this area over 15 years ago, many things had changed. There were new buildings, wider sidewalks, and pretty trees with Christmas lights decorated to give them a holiday spirit. Undoubtedly though, some things remained the same. "Mom, look over there! There are girls on the sidewalk. What are those women doing? It's the middle of the night!" the excited Nadia shouted out. Her nose pressed against the window. Natalia didn't reply and started to speed up.

"Mom, did you hear me? Do you know what these women are doing here in the middle of the freezing night? They are wearing weird clothes too. Are they homeless?"

"Yup, you can say that they are homeless!" Natalia finally answered. Her voice sounded unusually low.

"Mom, look, look." Nadia pointed her finger to the area on the right where the majority of the girls were standing. "There are lots of cars there, too. It must be some fun New Year's Eve tradition to go outside half-naked in the snow.

Those must all be a bunch of friends." Nadia added, still staring through the window, trying to guess what was going on. "Oh, wait, two women are getting into the back seat. They are laughing. I don't know what's going on over there. That's so weird, Mom. Are you sure they are homeless? Let's get closer and check it out."

Natalia was silent. Her patience was running low. Nadia had too much energy and asked way too many questions in the last few minutes. Natalia had no plans on answering any of them. She just tried to get out of that big street as soon as possible and kept a slow but steady pace. The girls on the sidewalk were now almost behind them.

"Mom, forget I asked. I'm stupid! It just came to me all of a sudden," said the upset Nadia. "Those women aren't homeless, and they are not having fun with their friends. I remember seeing these types in a scene in a movie. They are prostitutes! No, no, they are whores! They are disgusting lowlifes!" Nadia's hate was overwhelming. She had such passion and emotions in her words that one would think that those women did her wrong. "I would rather die than to even talk to one of them!" she added and turned to Natalia. "Mom, can you believe that they are doing this on New Year's Eve night? You do agree they are not human, don't you?" I mean, they sell their bodies! People can buy them like they can buy animals at the pet store. What a disgrace to our society!"

Natalia was in shock. She could not believe that Nadia was using such words. The poor woman was still silent, but now it was from astonishment of what the girl had just said. She didn't reply to Nadia and just pressed harder on the gas pedal. The second she speeded up, she heard a loud sound on the outside. Someone slammed a hand on the left side of the hood. Natalia braked the car as fast as she could, but it was too late. Whoever she almost drove over was already upset.

"Watch it, you fucking bitch! You almost killed me!"

Before Natalia could get out an apology, Nadia went off in a rage, like an animal that was kept chained up for a year and then let go. "Watch where you're going, you nasty whore! You better not have any dents on our car from your dirty hands! It's New Year's Eve! You shouldn't even be here! You are a low-life animal! Don't make me get out and fight you!" Nadia's eyes were on fire. She was unrecognizable and very aggressive. This outburst was a side of her that Natalia has never seen before.

The prostitute flipped them both off and walked around the car, continuing her way to the other side of the street. Natalia froze in place. Her body was pressing against the back of her seat, and her hands were squeezing the steering wheel like she was still trying to stop. Her eyes were open wide, and lips were tense. She couldn't believe the madness she just witnessed, especially coming from the 13-year-old girl she had adopted. To Natalia, it seemed like Nadia was angrier than the prostitute she had almost run over.

"Nadia, have you lost your mind?" finally asked Natalia. She was stunned and not in a good way. "Did you not see that it was completely my fault? I was the one who didn't pay attention to the road, and I was the one who almost ran over her. She did nothing wrong to deserve your aggression! On top of all that, how could you even say all those horrible things to any human being? Where did you hear all the vulgar words and how did you find so much hate in your heart? That woman is still a human, just like us!" Natalia was upset and hurt. She felt that Nadia acted entirely out of line.

She was not happy that Nadia had all that hate in her and it had never shown up until that moment. After all, Nadia had everything she ever wanted. Natalia gave her a good life and always taught her to be kind and understanding towards others. Still, after all that, there they were, in the car, with Nadia having a meltdown, screaming out one terrible thing after another.

"Mother! I can't believe you are saying that right now! Are you protecting that thing that hit our car? Are you saying that she is a person just like you and me, even though she sells her body and has sex with different men every day? Are you serious? I literally cannot believe you just said all that!"

"Nadia, even if you don't agree with me, it doesn't mean that you should be acting completely out of control. How do you even know why she is doing what she is doing? What if she is being forced to work on the streets?"

"Mother, if she didn't want to be here, she would have been doing something else to make that same money!"

"That's not true; not if she is forced to do this. I mean, did you take a closer look at her as she passed us? She didn't seem happy at all. She wasn't even wearing anything warm. I was even able to notice that she had a black eye and a ripped-up jacket! Does that sound like she wants to be on these streets, especially tonight? I am very disappointed in you, and it seems like you are not growing up to be a good human being!"

"Mother! Are you serious! Please, just forget about it! Get me out of here as soon as possible! I've had enough," snapped Nadia, taking off her shoes and putting up her feet underneath her. Then she placed her head down on her knees and in a rude gesture, covered her ears, showing Natalia that she didn't want to converse any longer.

Upset and troubled by what happened, Natalia started to drive away slowly. The shock from what had just transpired was overwhelming. Natalia's emotions were boiling up, but at the same time, she felt scared, anxious, and even mad for putting herself in that situation. She knew that when Nadia asked her to ride around the center, especially in this weather, the answer should have been a solid "no," but it wasn't.

Natalia was too overprotective of her new daughter and felt that because of it Nadia had full control of that situation. On the other hand, what just transpired, was a sign of how Nadia would react if she found out the truth about Natalia's past life. The famous saying that "everything happens for a reason" seemed to apply here.

About twenty minutes later Natalia made it to the building and pulled into the parking garage. Nadia was silent the whole ride back and stayed in the same exact position with her ears still covered. Natalia was also upset and didn't want to talk to Nadia either. The elevator ride was just as awkward, and Nadia stood with her back towards Natalia up until the doors opened.

When they got to the apartment, Nadia went straight to her room. Natalia didn't mind that at all and was even glad that she didn't have to converse or discuss everything that just happened.

She took off her shoes and went into the kitchen to get a fresh glass of cold water that she always had on the nightstand. The moment she poured the glass and turned around to leave the kitchen, she saw Nadia. The girl was standing a few feet away from Natalia, and her expression looked aggressive.

"I don't want to talk about what happened tonight," Nadia said. "I do, however, want to talk about a couple of things that you promised to discuss a few weeks ago." Nadia's hands crossed over her chest. She looked like an angry teacher talking to the student.

"Nadia, I'm pretty sure that tonight is not the best time to talk about the past or anything at all for that matter," answered Natalia with a stern and low voice. She wasn't going to communicate with Nadia about anything, at least not until Nadia was calm.

"No, you have said the same thing last time. It seems like there is never a good time to talk to you about anything. You are way too busy, too tired or just don't feel like it! Honestly, I'm getting very annoyed by this and starting not to trust you."

"Watch what you say!" answered Natalia. "I'm a grown woman and will not take any disrespect from you. You already said enough in the car. Now you come up to me and start to talk like I did you wrong. When people don't want to answer questions, it means they are not ready for them, and you should let it go."

"What are you talking about? How am I disrespectful to you? I'm just sick and tired of being like the doll that you can dress up and show off. If you considered me your true daughter or best friend, as you say we are, then you would answer any questions I ask! There wouldn't be any games that you are playing for the past few weeks!" The girl was yelling.

"Nadia, you are completely out of control. I don't know anything about your past other then what you already told me. I have no idea where your biological parents are or where to find them. I don't understand what you want from me."

"I'm not asking about my parents. I told you that I'm interested in things about you! I don't even know where you are from or where were you born! You have zero pictures of yourself up until five years ago and not one picture of anyone from your family. Don't you have some relatives, parents, siblings or childhood friends, or did you grow up in an orphanage like me? Do you think this is normal? Do you think you are normal?"

"That's enough! I've had it with you! You are getting more and more out of control. Stop now, or I will reprimand you!" loudly replied Natalia, slamming the glass on the counter so hard that half of the water spilled.

"Reprimand me? Oh, now you will punish me for wanting to know more about the woman who adopted me and with whom I live? That's just great! Go right ahead! I'm not afraid of you!"

"I wasn't trying to scare you! I simply am asking you to stop this argument or I will leave the apartment and sleep at my friend's house."

"Friend's house? You have no friends! But yeah, go ahead, leave! What a surprise! Leave me, just like my actual mother did! Maybe, if you hadn't adopted me, my mother would have come for me! I bet that by now she has changed her mind and now wants me back. I don't even need you! I'm going to find my birth parents anyways, as soon as I turn 18! I'm going to leave you! You can stay here and live alone with all of your secrets, like a big happy family!"

Natalia's eyes opened wide. Nadia's words were too painful for her to hear. She didn't expect such harsh mistreatment, especially from the only person Natalia let into her life. She looked down and slowly walked towards the hallway. Nadia wasn't saying anything. Her hands were still folded with an attitude as if she were ready to continue the fight but it was all over. Natalia made up her mind. Nadia's last few sentences said and showed her everything that she needed to see. Their living together was not going to work.

Natalia slowly grabbed her boots and put them on. She

then took her warm hat and winter coat off the hanger and unlocked the front door. Without any hesitation, she walked out of the apartment, and the door slowly closed shut behind her.

Even if she wanted to tell Nadia everything, she couldn't, not after what she saw half an hour earlier. If Nadia said all those horrifying things about the prostitute Natalia almost ran over, then what would she say about her adoptive mother. If Nadia knew about Natalia being locked up in a room and used for sex month after month, she would most likely not understand it. Even if Nadia accepted that fact, she would probably not have taken well to the idea that she had left her newborn baby to die. Most likely Nadia would not want to see Natalia at all for the rest of her life. Natalia realized that they couldn't continue living together. Again her faith was being tested.

When the door closed, angry Nadia locked it from the inside and went into the living room. She rarely stayed home alone, not to mention in the middle of the night. Nadia was brave but still nervous and yet didn't feel sorry for the hurtful things just said to her mother. She was a typical teenager: a 13-year-old girl, who didn't appreciate or understand how much her mother did for her on a daily basis.

Meanwhile, shocked and upset, Natalia went down to the garage and got into her car. Tears were silently streaming down her face. She realized that after everything she had given to this girl, it was still not enough. Nadia would never stop asking questions or dig for the answers, and Natalia knew very well that the girl wasn't able to handle the real truth. It was a dead end.

Tired, upset and disappointed, Natalia pulled out of the garage to take a ride on the empty streets and focus her thoughts. Her plan was, not to stay at her friend's house for the rest of the night or even go there. She just needed a little bit of time with smooth music and a slow but calming drive. At least those were her intentions when she got on the road.

The time was already approaching three in the morning. The street lights were still off, and the snowplows weren't out yet. Natalia decided to get on the highway where it was always lit up and less snowy. When she got on the main road, it looked pretty empty and already shoveled. All the lights were working, and the ride was smooth: precisely what Natalia wanted. Feeling good, she moved to the left lane pressing the gas pedal to get to full speed.

About ten minutes into driving, more and more cars got onto the highway. By now, Natalia felt like her head had cleared enough, and she would look for a resolution in the morning. She decided to end her night and to go back home. She quickly moved from lane to lane, trying to get all the way to the right and take the next exit so she could turn around.

As she slowly switched to the last lane before the exit, she saw bright head lights in the rearview mirror. They were approaching faster than she expected. She realized that her speed dropped too quickly and that she had waited too long to move over multiple lanes and make it into that exit. In the spur of the moment, Natalia decided to press the gas pedal as hard as she could, to gain the speed back up, but it was too late. The car didn't speed up fast enough.

The last thing she remembered was the ear-piercing sound of brakes and the force of the impact. The eighteen-wheel oil tanker hit the back of her car at a speed of at least 60 miles an hour. The effect was massive. Natalia's airbags immediately inflated and her vehicle flew up in the air.

A second later, her car dropped back onto the highway and flipped over and over at least five times. Finally, it landed upside down, looking like it went through a heavy-duty pressing machine. The spot of the crash was about ten feet away from the very exit she was trying to take to get back home.

Natalia was unconscious. Her head was pressing against the roof and blood was dripping from somewhere under her hair. The massive impact also jammed both of her legs under the dashboard, and both of her arms looked broken. There was no doubt that Natalia's stressful New Year's Eve was now over.

CHAPTER ELEVEN

H ello?"

"Is this Nadejda Lebedeva?"

"Yes, this is Nadia. Who is this?"

"I'm an ER surgeon, calling you from the Central Hospital Emergency Room. It's about your mother."

"My mother? Why? What happened? Is she ok?"

"No, she isn't. She has been in a bad accident but survived. She is in surgery now, and we are doing the best we can to save her, but things aren't looking too promising."

"No! Oh my God! Is this a joke?" Nadia started to cry out loud, screaming like she was a wounded animal.

"Please calm down. We need you to come to the hospital!"

"I don't want my mommy to die. Doctor, please!"

"We are trying to save her, but you still need to come here as soon as you can. Your mother has only you listed in all of her medical records. Are there any other adults in the house?"

"No, it's just the two of us. We don't have anyone else. It's all my fault. I was so mean to my mom tonight! I didn't mean it! She can't die! You will make sure she makes it, right?"

"As I said, we are doing our best. Your mother has multiple injuries and internal bleeding. She also has a broken skull, leg, both arms, a couple of ribs, as well a punctured left lung. Do you have anyone who can bring you here?"

"No, my mom is the only person I have!"

"Ok, ok, let me think. I will send the ambulance to get you right now. We have your address. Go outside in 15 minutes."

"Ok, I'll be waiting. Please go save my mom!"

"We will do what we can. Just don't get your hopes up. I don't want you to be more upset than you are now because I misled you. Even if we save your mother, she will never function normally again. She hasn't gained consciousness since we got her. Plus, there is only a five percent chance she can make it out of this surgery. If she does, then she will probably have to be kept alive by mechanical machines. Her lungs and brain are both damaged. Most importantly the chance of her ever coming out of the coma is practically zero."

Nadia slammed the phone down and dropped to her knees. Her life as she knew it was over. Within seconds, the realization of how wrong it was to push Natalia to that point, took over Nadia. Only now she understood how selfish her behavior was towards the only person who loved her unconditionally. If Natalia survived the surgery but stayed in a coma, Nadia was doomed. Her life was going to become darker than it had ever been. The nightmare was here.

Nadia concentrated her thoughts. She got up, put on her shoes, walked to the closet and grabbed her coat off the hanger. Before leaving the apartment, Nadia gave it another look. For the first time in many years, she was scared. A strange feeling of loneliness was seeping into her with every passing second.

Suddenly she ran into her bedroom and started to search through the old box in the closet. A minute later Nadia found what she was seeking. It was her doll, the Babaika, the one she hadn't touched since the day she moved there. Nadia put the Babaika into her pocket, walked out of the apartment and locked the door. Nadia knew it was still a few minutes too early, but it didn't matter because she felt safer outside than inside.

The night was very dark. The lights around the buildings were working, but she couldn't see farther than their glow. Fortunately a couple of minutes later, the headlights of the ambulance showed up in the distance. Another few moments and the vehicle pulled up. A nurse came out of the passenger seat and opened the back door, waving to Nadia to get in quickly.

A minute later they were on their way to the hospital. Nadia was very anxious. She hated not knowing what was going on.

"Excuse me, nurse? Do you know how my mom is doing?"

"No, I do not," answered the middle-aged woman in a clipped voice.

"Excuse me, sir," Nadia tried asking the driver. "Do you know anything about my mother?"

"Sorry, I don't know anything either. I wasn't the responder to that call," he replied.

The second the ambulance pulled up, Nadia squeezed Babaika which was still in her pocket and came up to the door. She was waiting for the nurse to unlock it and when the door opened Nadia jumped out. She started to run towards the emergency room entrance as if her life depended on it.

The moment she got inside, Nadia looked around

frantically. One of the nurses saw her and came over. "Who are you looking for?"

"My mom, whose name is Natalia Lebedeva. Do you know where she is?"

"Yes, I do. Your mother is still in the operating room. It will be a while, so you should go to the waiting area. We'll come and get you when she is in recovery."

"Thank you. I'll be in the waiting room," answered Nadia.

The nurse left, and Nadia slowly walked over to the waiting area. It was empty and quiet. The first night of the New Year must not have been that busy for the ER. People were still partying. Nadia found the best spot in the far corner, sat down and rested her head against the wall.

Nadia couldn't turn back the hands of time, but she wished she could. The girl felt terrible and was taking full responsibility for what had happened to Natalia. At this point, it was unknown if she was ever going to see her mother again. The only thing she could now do was to pray.

A few minutes later, the tired and scared Nadia fell asleep. She didn't remember having any dreams, but four hours later someone's hand gently rocked her, and she woke up. It was the doctor.

"Nadia? I spoke with you over the phone. I'm doctor Lekarstvin. The surgery is over, and your mom made it."

"Yes! Yes! Thank you, God! I knew it! I knew she would!"

"Well, it surely is terrific news! She is a fighter and has a healthy heart; however, do you recall our phone conversation?"

"Yes, what part of it are you referring to?"

"I'm talking about the coma that your mother is in."

"Oh yes, I do recall you talking about it. It's like sleep, right?"

"Yes and no. Your mother is asleep but will never wake up."

"What do you mean never? Like until she is 100 years old?"

"I don't know when, but as long as she is alive, she will be in a coma. Your mother is in what we call a persistent vegetative state. Plus, part of her lungs got damaged when a couple of her ribs broke, so right now we have her hooked up to a breathing machine."

"What if she can breathe on her own at some point?"

"Well, then, we can disconnect the machine but will have yet another problem. Your mother's brain was also injured when she broke her skull, and it took much longer for us to stop the bleeding than we expected. We are all agreed that she is in a permanent coma and is going to sleep forever, Nadia. I am very sorry."

"Hmm, I'm still pretty sure she is going to wake up."

"Ok. Well, I can't stop you from hoping for the best. I do need to tell you that we can only keep your mother at the hospital for ninety days."

"What do you mean for ninety days?"

"If she is still in a coma, we can't continue her life support after midnight of day ninety. It's the law."

"Are you saying that if she doesn't wake up by midnight at the end of day ninety, you will disconnect the machines?"

"Yes, that's the law. Some of the comatose patients we had would probably live for decades. We can't afford to support them that long unless relatives pay out of pocket on day ninety-one and on."

"Well, today is just day one, so there. Now I'd like to see my mother please!"

Nadia was pissed off, and her voice was sarcastic. The doctor motioned her to follow him, and they went into the restricted area. She walked behind him as they passed the recovery rooms and went through an extensive corridor. A moment later they got to the part of the hospital where there were patients who had unusual conditions.

When they walked up to room number 11, the door was half open. The doctor pointed to it and motioned for Nadia to go in. She looked at him a little surprised, but he broke their eye contact and walked away. Nadia entered the room. When she saw her mother, Nadia slowly dropped Babaika from her hand. The nervous girl took a couple of small steps forward and covered her mouth with the palm of her hand. She was shocked to see her mother in such a terrible condition.

Natalia had bandages everywhere from head to toe. Her right leg and both of her arms were in casts, suspended in the air. Her head was also tightly wrapped, as well as her chest. It was a heartbreaking sight.

Nadia looked to the right and saw the breathing machine pumping air through the mask on her mother's face. Natalia seemed so peaceful and tranquil. Nadia was getting emotional. There were so many things that she wanted to talk to her mother about but realized that Natalia now couldn't even reply.

The doctor walked in a moment later and came up to the right side of Natalia's bed. He checked the two monitors near the headboard and wrote down some numbers. Nadia was watching.

"Her vital signs are all good. Now she just needs to rest and heal. One of my nurses will take you home in half an hour."

"Oh no, I'm not going home. No, I'm staying right here!"

"You can't stay here. There is only a small recliner for brief rests and don't you have to go to school anyway?"

Forgive Me, Nadia

"Doctor, I'm a high honors student, and I am not going back to school until my mom is the one bringing me there. The teachers won't mind. Trust me, they all love me. I am going to sleep right here." Nadia was very stern and made the doctor understand how adamant she was about what she just said.

"Fine, it's your choice. If you want to stay here without a TV, clothes, friends, and good food, then go ahead. Be my guest."

"Thank you very much. I just want to be here when my mother wakes up, that's all."

The doctor shook his head and walked away. He knew that it wasn't going to be an easy case and felt terrible that Nadia was setting herself up for disappointment. He told all of his nurses to make sure that Nadia was getting food and whatever else she needed. The doctor knew that the poor thing didn't understand the severity of what was going on.

From that night on, Natalia didn't leave her mother's room even for a day. A week later, a couple of Natalia's co-workers stopped by the hospital and dropped off her work laptop and some clothes for Nadia. After that, they came by every other week to take the dirty clothes and get it washed. At least they helped.

Nadia was living at the hospital. She took showers at the nurses wash-up room, ate by her mother's side, and did her school work on Natalia's laptop. All the nurses loved Nadia. She was now a changed girl. That night on New Year's Eve completely changed her perspective on life and rearranged her values.

A month later Natalia's mask came off, and the doctor said that she was able to now breathe on her own. Still, there were no signs of her waking up. Not even one. Again, it didn't faze Nadia, and she had no plans on giving up.

187

As time went one, day ninety was slowly approaching. Nadia had been praying by her mother's side every morning and night. She talked to Natalia all day long and told her many funny stories about her life in the orphanage. She also asked Natalia numerous times to give her another chance and to wake up.

The nurses and doctors gave up on explaining to Nadia that her mother could not hear her. The stubborn girl just didn't want to listen. On top of that, she didn't even consider going home, despite numerous attempts by the staff to talk her into that.

When month three was coming to an end, a couple of social workers walked into the room. Nadia was doing her homework while humming a melody. The social workers looked at each other in confusion.

The atmosphere was so alive that no one would even guess that there was a patient in that room, never mind in a coma. Nadia had taped different drawings she made on all the walls and decorated the room with whatever she was able to get in the hospital. The creative girl found a scented battery-operated candle in one of the empty hospital rooms and brought it in as well. The light was giving out a fresh smell of strawberries. To top the scene off, Natalia was peacefully lying on her bed without bandages on any parts of her body.

Everything just looked so different from what the social workers expected. One of them stepped out of the room and looked up at the number on the door. She wanted to make sure that they came to the right place. They did.

"Are you Nadia Lebedeva?"

"Yes, I am. How can I help you?"

"We are here to speak with you. We work for child services and are in charge of your case. We need to explain to you what's going to happen a couple of weeks from now."

"Ok, sure. Go ahead. I just finished my homework."

"Ok, great. Here are our business cards, just in case you need to get hold of us before March 31st."

"Thank you, but why would I need to call you at all?"

"Well, didn't anyone explain to you what happens on day ninety-one? The head doctor told us that he spoke to you."

"Yes, he did tell me that the hospital can only keep my mom until midnight on day ninety. I guess what he was trying to say is that at 12:00 a.m. on April 1st they have to disconnect her food supply and all other equipment. That supposedly will slowly kill her, so if that's what you are referring to then sure, the doctor did speak to me about it, but I'm not worried. They are doctors, and their job is to save lives! They don't kill their patients, especially my mom, not to mention on her birthday!"

The social workers looked at each other and shook their heads. They felt terrible that Nadia was so hopeful and that she believed in the impossible. It was like she was still in denial. One of the social workers pulled out some paperwork and looked up.

"Nadia, we are not here on behalf of your mother's life support. We are here for you."

"You are here for me? What do you mean?"

"By law, you have to be of legal age to live on your own, and you are nowhere close to that. You can't stay by yourself in the condo until you turn eighteen. We are very sorry."

Nadia was confused. What they were saying didn't sound right. It seemed like they wanted to take her elsewhere.

"So, I'm confused. What exactly are you saying?"

"What we are saying is that if your mother doesn't wake up by midnight on March 31st, you will have to go to an orphanage if there is a spot available or into a foster home. We can assure you that none of your mother's stuff will be touched. Your mother's lawyer will sign everything over to you as soon as you are of legal age."

Nadia's eyes opened wide. She angrily closed the laptop and got up, walking up to the women. They were a bit confused on what she was going to do, but Nadia just walked right past them and went out of the room. The social workers waited ten minutes for Nadia to return and when she didn't, they left as well.

When the aggravated girl came back a half hour later, she closed the door and came up to her mother's bed. She dropped down to her knees and covered her face with both hands. She started to cry. The distraught girl was now even more upset.

For the next few days, Nadia didn't even eat. She didn't do any homework, didn't take a shower and didn't talk. She was falling apart. An unbreakable little girl was trying hard to hold on to her weak faith.

Every night she fell asleep on her mother's bed, right next to her feet. Every morning with sadness, she crossed off another day on the big calendar on the wall. With each X she put on it, her fear grew stronger and more powerful. Nothing looked good.

Even her prayers were not full of emotions anymore. She was never big into them in the first place, although she started to believe in God after that day on the train when she found Natalia. The first real heart-felt prayer she said was while she sat in the waiting room of the hospital after her mother's accident.

Now, even though God had yet to answer her prayers, it was the only way she was able to stay sane. She prayed out loud every single morning and every single night. She asked the Universe, the God and any other higher powers above for help in waking her mother up. All the while, the peaceful Natalia just lay there calm and quiet, with her life entirely in God's hands.

March 31st seemed to come very fast and the traffic in and out of the room throughout the day was non-stop. The doctors, the nurses, a lawyer, and even the police, all entered and left at one point or another. Nadia couldn't stand it. She wasn't talking to anyone or even acknowledging them and made no effort to move out of their way.

By the evening, Nadia noticed that the traffic had slowed down and now only a couple of nurses randomly peeked in to check up on her. They looked sad, and no one was saying anything. The doctor popped in for just a moment during the evening.

By now, Nadia was a total mess. She moved up from the bottom of the bed to now lying by her mother's side. Nadia's head was on top of Natalia's stomach, and she wrapped her arms around her mother. The poor girl felt so lost and was continuously crying.

Around 10:30 p.m., the doctor stopped by to check on Nadia. The girl only looked up once, when he first walked over to the other side of the bed. He seemed to be emotional as well even though he had seen a lot in his career. It was apparent that these types of situations were very disturbing to him.

"You will be ok! Do you understand? I don't know how but I have a powerful feeling, that you will be just fine," he said and touched Nadia's hair. She nodded at him and closed her eyes. The doctor sadly left the room. It was a beautiful gesture on his part to make Nadia feel better. After all, he was a human being and had feelings.

The clock on the wall above Natalia's bed was ticking, and it seemed like the second hand was going faster than usual. It was now 11 p.m., and Nadia's heart was beating faster and faster. It was still just the two of them in the room so the girl decided to tell Natalia how she felt, almost like confessions but with the sincere hope that Natalia could somehow hear her. The poor girl just wanted her mother's forgiveness.

"Mom, I am so sorry for everything that happened. I truly am." She was sobbing. "If I could turn the time around, I would never disobey you or argue with you! I know you wanted what's best for me and I was a fool to think that I knew any better. I should have cherished our time together instead of neglecting and disrespecting you. If you can hear me right now, please forgive me!"

Even at this point, three months later, Nadia still had a naive hope that her mother could wake up. The brave girl just didn't want to give up. She believed in miracles and had pure faith. She was only a child, who was afraid to experience the unfairness that life could give.

With sorrow in her heart and tears in her eyes, she felt desperate. She wanted to give it her all. "Mom, if you can hear me, I want you to know that I need you to wake up right now! I need you more than ever! In less than an hour from now, the doctors will disconnect the remaining machines, and you will slowly go to heaven. I don't want you to go! I love you very much! I want you to know that if I could pick any mother in the world before I was born, I would have picked you, and only you. I just don't want to live without you." Nadia closed her eyes and slowly placed her head back down on her mother's stomach. A few minutes later she drifted off into a beautiful dream: the one that she wished was an actual reality.

In it, she saw Natalia awake, with a loving smile and a happy face. Her eyes were sparkling. She was looking at Nadia in complete silence. Nadia wasn't crying. She was soaking in the realistic feeling of her mother's presence. It felt hopeful and magical. Everything in that dream felt so perfect and real. Even the room, the bed, and the clock all looked vaguely familiar. It was like being in a fairy tale, not just a dream.

"Nadia! Nadia! Nadia, move away from the bed, right now," screamed a nervous nurse. She was standing right behind Nadia. "Doctor, doctor hurry!" she yelled out even louder. She was trying to get others into the room.

Nadia turned her head and looked up at the nurse in a confused and aggravated manner. She was mad that the nurse had just interrupted such a fantastic dream she was having. The annoyed girl looked at the nurse with pure anger. After giving the nurse an irritated look, Nadia decided to go back into her beautiful dream.

Just before she closed her eyes, she glanced up at her mother and got a shock. The poor girl's head began to spin, and she became lightheaded. A moment later, scared Nadia quickly moved away from the bed and into the furthest corner of the room. She put her head down and covered her face with both hands like she had seen a ghost. The room was so silent that both Nadia's and Natalia's breathing was the only sound of life in it. The nurse was out looking for others, and Nadia was still in the corner, her hands covering the face.

A minute later three nurses and an on-call doctor walked in. They rushed to the bed, hovering over Natalia. The doctor was trying to take the vital signs, while nurses were turning back on the breathing machine. Nadia was too afraid to look up.

When the doctor who was on call dialed the phone and

asked the head doctor to come into the hospital as soon as possible, Nadia started to get curious. She uncovered her face and looked up. It took her a few seconds to understand what was going on. Everything was happening too fast and too confusing for her to comprehend. She distinctly remembered falling asleep and then dreaming about her mother, so things weren't making any sense.

There she was, across the room looking at the bed and her mother was looking right back at her with that same loving smile that she just saw in the dream. The beautiful blue eyes, staring at her, were overflowing with love and kindness. Nadia was lost and confused as if she were still asleep. Was this just a dream or was it real? The look that Natalia had in her eyes at that very moment was just like the first time they met on that train. Only this time her eyes didn't have a shocking stare in them. The way she was looking back at Nadia was genuine, pure, and compassionate.

Natalia was out of the coma. Unbelievably and by an entirely incredible miracle, she indeed was awake. The doctor raised the head of her bed half-way up, and she was now able to observe the people around her. Of course, the first person that got Natalia's attention was Nadia. The poor girl was still shocked and seemed to be talking to herself. "It's not a dream, is it?" Nadia whispered under her breath. She was asking herself the question as if she were the only believable person at that moment. "It is a reality, right?"

"What is the time? Oh my God, the time. What time is it? Is it too late? Is it after midnight?" the poor girl anxiously screamed out loud. Her eyes were urgently searching for the clock, forgetting that it was on the same wall and in the same spot as it had been for the past three months. She just wasn't thinking clearly. Naively, Nadia still thought that if it was now after midnight, her mother was going away. She found the clock and took a deep breath, letting out all of her frightened feelings.

"It's not midnight! It's only 11:11! Wait, what, only 11:11? Did I fall asleep only a few minutes ago? Did I even fall asleep at all? I'm mixed up about all this!"

Nadia was out of control, asking herself one question after another. A few seconds later, one of the nurses realized that the girl was in a bewildered state of mind and walked up to her. Nadia stopped talking and looked wide-eyed at the nurse.

"Nadia, it's all going to be ok!" Just relax. You are going to be all right!" The nurse was smiling. She loved Nadia, just like everyone at that hospital did. "Do you see what just happened? It's a miracle! God answered your prayers! He helped you! He saw how strong your faith was and rewarded you with exactly what you asked! I hope you know that this happened because you never gave up. You had more belief than all of us combined! You are simply amazing."

She hugged Nadia and helped her up. The poor girl was shaking. The nurses slowly walked Nadia toward the bed. Her eyes still were locked on her mother. With every small step, the reality of it all being real was more evident.

She walked a little closer, let go of the nurse's hand and rushed to her mother as fast as she could. The happy Nadia wrapped her arms around Natalia's neck and started to cry with her face on her mother's chest. "Mommy! You came back! My mommy! You didn't give up! You didn't leave me! I knew it! I just knew it! I love you! Sorry for everything I did wrong! I have so much to tell you! Oh, my God, I can't believe this!" Nadia's cry was so genuine and sincere that every single person in that room started to cry, even the doctor who up to now had tried his best to hide his real emotions.

Natalia gently pulled Nadia's face up towards hers and kissed her on the cheek. "Sweetie, no more crying, ok? You've cried enough. It's time to celebrate." Her voice was so clear and heartwarming. She wanted to calm Nadia down and make her feel comfortable with what had just happened. "Sweetie, I tried moving many times but I just couldn't. I heard every single word that you and the other people who were visiting were saying. When the social workers came by last week and said that you would be going back into the system, I had to do something about it. I had to come out of the coma or both of our lives would have ended."

"Mom? How were you able to finally wake up?"

"I don't even know how. I just continued praying in my head, over and over again, begging God and the Universe to give me another chance. I visualized daily us being together and going for a walk in the park. I pictured and remembered all of the fun times we had, and I continued concentrating only on good things that I had in my life. I used the deepest corners of my heart and my soul to come back and now here I am, back with you." She smiled.

"Mom, you are amazing! You are the best mother anyone could ever have! You are so strong and powerful that nothing can stop you, even that stupid coma! Oh, and happy upcoming birthday!

I know! I know! It's crazy how life works. I was counting the days along with you. I don't think I was even in a full coma. My mind was fully aware of everything around me as soon as the doctors brought me into this room. I just couldn't move any parts of my body or open my eyes."

Forgive Me, Nadia

.   .   .

A week later, Natalia had made a full recovery and was able to go home. As for Nadia, she was a changed girl. She became kind, polite, respectful, and genuinely appreciative of every single thing Natalia did for her.

When Nadia's 14th birthday came, Natalia organized a big celebration. Nadia was happy and thankful. She didn't ask for any presents or anything else. Of course, she still got dozens of gifts with the biggest of them yet to come the very next morning.

"Hey, sleepyhead, wake up and get dressed quickly," said Natalia peeking her head into Nadia's bedroom.

"Ma, it's too early, and besides it's a Sunday!"

"I know, but you are going to love where we are going."

"Alright! I'm getting up. I'll be ready in ten minutes."

"Ok and don't pack anything. We'll be back later on tonight."

"Ok. Oh, mom, you know what I think I am going to do?" Nadia tossed her blanket aside and sat up on the bed facing Natalia. "I know you don't like it when I use my phone while we are out, so I'm going to leave it here in my room!"

"Wow! Thank you, sweetie! You are such a good girl!"

"Yup, that's me! You and I come first, then the rest of the world," said Nadia with a smile. She then grabbed her phone and raised it up in the air. "Look, mom, I am turning it off." She pressed the power button, and the phone went dark.

About fifteen minutes later they were ready to go and left the condo. Nadia had no idea what surprise her mother had for her and Natalia gave no clues; at least not until they got in the car and she drove them to the central train station.

"Mom, are we going on vacation? I have finals at school starting tomorrow morning." Nadia raised her eyebrows.

"No! It's not a vacation! It's just a little surprise. It's something that you asked me about in the past."

"Me? I didn't ask you to go anywhere!" Nadia was intrigued.

"Yes, you did, not right out, but in other ways you did."

"Oh? Ok, let me guess. Hmmm, how far away is it?"

"It will probably be about a two-hour train ride."

"Oh my God, I think I know! You want to go back to Daisy?"

"Yup, you got it! You wanted to know where you were born and who your biological parents are. Well, let's go find out."

"Wow. Mom, now that is a real surprise! You are too cute!"

"I know, I know!" Natalia smiled. "You wanted this for a while so let's go and get it out of the way!"

They parked the car and got the tickets. The train showed up twenty minutes later. Even though this train ride should have been much different from the last one they took together, it was very similar. Just like then, there were many uncertainties about what was going to happen next. Was Natalia going to be able to get any information from the orphanage? Were they going to find Nadia's biological parents? What if they were sorry and wanted Nadia back?

Thinking about all of those things made for a quiet train ride. Both Nadia and Natalia had their fears. This trip was bittersweet, but one thing was for sure by now, they were inseparable best friends.

When the train arrived at Pavlovo, and they came out into the train station, Nadia started to feel some fear, and in some strange way, she felt powerless. After all, the fact of her running away from Daisy was still there. She had no idea if she might get in trouble for it or if the authorities would take her from Natalia.

"Mom, when we get there, I'm going to wait outside."

"Sure, no problem, whatever you want to do."

Natalia got a taxi, and the two of them headed to Daisy.

Nadia was looking outside and admiring the beautiful May flowers that Mother Nature had provided. She also noticed how many things around the village had changed. There were many new roads and buildings here now. Pavlovo had turned into a cute little city. As Nadia noticed dozens of luxury cars passing by, her curiosity got the best of her.

"Excuse me, sir," she said to the driver. "I haven't been here for a while, but I couldn't help but notice how much Pavlovo has changed. What's going on?"

"Oh yeah, lots of new roads and buildings are getting built here. We even have our bank branch and a mini shopping center, and now we don't have to go to Moscow for every little thing."

"Wow, that's awesome! I bet people who live here love that!"

"Well, yes and no. We love the new changes, but the crime rate went up too. Just about every week people get robbed, kidnapped, or their cars get stolen."

"Wow, that's not good. I guess people have to be careful."

The driver nodded his head and continued driving. Less than forty-five minutes later, the taxi pulled up right in front of the orphanage. Natalia paid him and took down his information so she could call him for a ride back to the train station. He left, and now both Natalia and Nadia were standing in front of the building.

"Mom, Daisy looks so different from before. It's bigger and wider. This road wasn't even here back then. Now, it's nice, flat, and connected to the main route. The playground is brand new and look; there are even benches where people can relax."

"That is nice. I'm glad this place got a makeover. I don't want to waste more time, so let me go in. I'll be quick!"

Natalia smiled and walked toward the entrance. Nadia looked around to see how she could entertain herself. Most of the kids her age used modern technology of some sort to pass the time.

Now, she had to figure out how not to be bored. Nadia decided to stay busy in an old-fashioned way; by checking out new things around the building and just admiring Mother Nature.

Meanwhile, Natalia buzzed the front door. Someone on the other side asked her what the purpose of her visit was and Natalia replied that she was there to speak to the director. The director coming there on a Sunday was hit or miss. Natalia was lucky. He was there. A moment later she was buzzed in, and Natalia walked right into the front foyer.

One of the teachers greeted her with a smile and showed her the way to the director's office. She must have thought that Natalia was there to adopt one of the kids but wasn't entirely sure. "Do you have an appointment with Mr. Petrovich? He is usually not here on Sundays, and we were all surprised that he came in, so it was probably for you," said the teacher as they walked down the corridor.

"Yes, he must have come just for me," replied Natalia.

"Ok. Well, whatever it is, good luck."

They walked up to the director's door, and the teacher knocked. "Mr. Petrovich, your appointment is here."

"Who?" replied the director from the other side. He sounded drunk and confused.

"Your appointment, sir. Didn't you set one up for today?"

"I did? I don't remember, but ok, its fine, I'll take it."

The teacher pushed open the door, letting Natalia in and walked away.

"Hello, what can I help you?" asked the director. His nose was red as if someone had kissed the tip of it with bright red lipstick. His right hand was shaking while holding a large bottle of vodka. He was pouring right into a tall champagne glass, and Natalia's presence there didn't make him pause. She was confused about why he wasn't hiding his drinking habit from anyone at work, but she quickly realized that he was already drunk.

"Hi, my name is Natalia Lebedeva." She introduced herself confidently but didn't extend her hand, in case he was going to use that same hand and possibly drop the bottle by mistake. She continued, "I am here to talk about a little girl who ran away from this orphanage three years ago. Her name is Nadia."

When the director heard the name, his hand that was holding the bottle started to shake. He looked into Natalia's eyes and immediately put the vodka back on his desk. He was confused and fearful. He had no idea if Natalia was there to ask questions or if she had information that he didn't have.

"What about her?" he asked and sat down in his chair.

"Well, first of all, she is safe and has been living with me ever since the day she ran away from here. I found her at the train station. She had nowhere to go, so I decided to adopt her."

"Thank you, God!" The director took a deep breath and looked up at the ceiling. "I'm glad she is ok. We reported her missing the next day, but I'm not sure if anyone started to work on her case."

"That is sad, but I am glad to say that I'm the adoptive parent and Nadia is doing great! The reason I'm here is that both of us still have many unanswered questions."

The director's facial expression changed, and he became serious. He took a professional pose and quickly placed the bottle of vodka on the floor. "Ms. Lebedeva, I am sure you are very well aware of the privacy laws. Unfortunately, I cannot discuss any information about our children unless you have a court order allowing me to do so. Please accept my apologies."

"Oh, is that right?" Natalia replied with sarcasm. "I find it funny how you stick to the rules, yet here you are drunk at your office, especially in the orphanage. Is that something that's allowed around here? Do you have a court order for that?"

"How dare you blackmail me? I am not drunk, and I only came here for a couple of hours because my wife and I were arguing at the house! I needed my space."

"Oh, so you came here to get drunk? That's nice. Hey, are you going to drive home in this condition as well? I'm just curious."

"OK! Enough! Just tell me what you want to know."

"Nadia told me that her alcoholic parents brought her to Daisy a few days after she was born. She overheard some teachers talk about it. All we want to know now is the names of her parents." The director kept looking back and forth between Natalia and the bottle. He couldn't wait for her to leave so he could drink more of it. "Ok, you want to know where she came from, fine, but make sure no one knows that I revealed that information to you."

Natalia nodded, silently telling the director that he shouldn't worry. Feeling that he could trust her, he opened the top drawer of his desk and pulled out a small key. Then he slowly got up and started to walk towards the far corner of his office. There, Natalia saw a tall metal filing cabinet. That is where they kept all the files for every single child who had ever lived in that orphanage.

As the director was making his way to the files, Natalia was trying not to laugh. It was amusing to watch how he was barely able to stay on his feet and was wobbling from side to side. His arms were spread up in the air, and he was trying to control his balance. It was funnier than watching someone who is very drunk trying to walk a straight line.

When he finally made it to the cabinet, he unlocked the third drawer down. The label on it said "L-Q." He found Nadia's file and pulled it out, quickly locking the door again.

"We have everyone's files under the last name, but Nadia's is under letter 'N' since she is the only one without a last name."

He said it loudly while trying to make his way back to the desk without falling.

"What do you mean she has no last name? How is that even possible? What about her parents' last name?"

"Well, here is the thing, Ms. Lebedeva," he replied as he dropped into his wide leather chair. "She doesn't even have a name because we don't know who her parents are. She got here under somewhat unusual circumstances."

"Wait a minute; I'm confused. Are you telling me that Nadia wasn't brought here by a mother or a father?"

"That is correct."

Natalia's eyes opened wide. She was bewildered and scared at the same time. What she heard was making her dizzy. She had to sit down in the chair next to her because she was about to faint. She could hardly concentrate, but somehow she managed to ask another question.

"So, if she doesn't have parents and you don't know where she is from, then how did she get here and when?"

The director carefully opened Nadia's file. It was thin. He bent the top of it towards him, so Natalia couldn't see the notes or whatever else was inside of it. He quickly refreshed his memory by reading a few things from the file and looked up.

"Well, the people from child services were the ones who brought her to us. She was a beautiful little thing, about two weeks old. I remember it now because we rarely get a newborn with a full head of hair and bright blue eyes. You know what? Her eyes looked a lot like yours."

The director paused for a moment and then went back to a professional manner of speaking. "But anyway, so what the social workers said is that some old man, who cleans the Moscow alleys during the night, heard a newborn crying in the distance. He followed the cry that led him to the double-dumpster. There in the left side of it, he discovered a baby wrapped in nothing but a dirty blanket. He picked her up and brought her to the hospital. She spent a couple of weeks there in recovery and then came to us. That is all I know about Nadia."

Natalia was staring wide-eyed at the director. She was as pale as a ghost and seemed to be barely breathing. All of a sudden she got up and grabbed the file out of the director's hands. An old small stained piece of wallpaper fell out of it and landed on the floor next to her foot. Natalia quickly grabbed it and looked at it. It had the word "Nadia" scratched on it. The letters were barely readable, but she knew what it was.

Natalia looked up at the director with shocked eyes and ran out of the office like a crazy person who had just escaped from an asylum. The director didn't say a word. He was astonished and didn't even try to stop her.

Natalia ran through the corridor as if the orphanage was on fire. She made it to the main foyer and came up to the front door. She was holding on to the file with both hands and used the right side of her body to push the door open.

When she got outside, Nadia wasn't in sight. She wasn't at the playground or on any of the benches. Natalia quickly looked around but still didn't see her. She decided to call her name and didn't care that someone from Daisy could hear it.

"Nadia! Nadia!" Natalia called loudly. She was getting more and more nervous and kept calling her name, but getting no reply.

When she didn't get any response, Natalia ran through the gate and onto the main road. The moment she stepped onto the street, she heard the squealing of tires and a girl's scream somewhere in the distance. She turned around and looked to the other side of the main road from where those sounds were coming.

There was a massive cloud of dust and smoke about a

hundred feet away from the gate. It was hard to make out what was going on. Natalia's instinct was to run towards the cloud, and as she did, the white van was now visible to her. It was speeding up and away, from her and the orphanage. She abruptly stopped in confusion. A horrifying flashback came to her mind. That van looked so familiar. She knew that she had seen one like it before.

Natalia's memory didn't take long to kick in. It was the same type of van that came to her the day before she turned fourteen. It belonged to the same organization to which her parents had sold her. The men that came to drug her and take her into sex-slavery had a van just like that.

The picture was now clear. The organization, by some cruel twist of fate, took her precious little angel. They just kidnapped her beautiful daughter, all while under her watch. She couldn't even tell Nadia that she was her birth mother. Natalia lost her child before she was able to confess and beg for mercy.

The poor woman started to panic, dropped to her knees on the road and cried frantically. It was that one time in which Natalia regretted not making Nadia take her phone with her. Now her brave but naïve little girl was gone, just like her mother at the same exact age. She was about to learn the hardships of teenage girls around the world who were kidnapped and abused. Nadia's destiny was now unknown and how long she had to live was entirely up to God.

VERONIKA GASPARYAN

CHAPTER 12

Natalia decided not to go to the police. Upon arrival back in Moscow, she got her emotions under control. She decided to come up with an immediate plan. It was irrational and outrageous, but it had to be insane for it to work. Natalia planned on rescuing her little girl on her own.

She knew that the police would not help. The kidnapping of young girls, especially those around fourteen years of age, happened dozens of times each month. It was happening not only in Moscow and its nearby regions of the city but also all around the country. Most of those cases were never solved. There were too many politicians and people in the justice system who had a significant financial gain from sex-trafficking. If confronted, they would just turn their heads away.

Natalia thought of a few options, but they all involved help from the police or other legal groups. The only thing that she could do without outside assistance was for her to go back into the organization, this time voluntarily. She had to go in as an undercover prostitute.

The desperate mother had to act fast. Every minute she waited, Nadia was getting abused, both physically and emotionally. Natalia was not unrealistic. She was just very well aware that by now her daughter had already experienced drugs, rape, and force. At the same time, Natalia knew that little Nadia had a powerful mind and a lot of strength. Nadia never gave up on her mother during the three months Natalia was in a coma. There was no way that Natalia was going to give up on her little girl now.

The very next morning Natalia went to her boss. She told him that she was having troubles with Nadia and needed time off immediately. Luckily for her, she had trained many others at the company, and her boss had no issues letting her take all the time she needed.

Later that day she contacted one of her clients she knew, who had connections with an illegally operated business that falsified documents. He told her where to go, what to do, and whom to see if she needed a complete identity change. Natalia learned very quickly how to be street smart, and within a few hours, she had a new last name. She ended up keeping her first name. That was ok to do since it was the most popular name in Russia, and at least a third of all the working girls were named Natalia.

Her next step was to get familiar with the locations and the pimps, so, for the next few days, Natalia concentrated on that part of the plan. She dressed up in provocative outfits and took a taxi to the nearest and the busiest sites where the prostitutes usually hang out. She narrowed down the few locations to the one specific spot that seemed to be the most active.

Natalia observed the girls, the customers, and the pimps by

sitting on the bench near that spot. Every night she stayed around until way after midnight. She was trying to catch the attention of the pimps without coming up to them. It was the first step in getting herself into the organization.

After three days, some of the clients pulling up noticed Natalia even before the pimps paid any attention to her. One by one the cars pulled up, and the guys invited her into their vehicles. She declined all of them but made sure that there was a quick dialog between them. Natalia did that on purpose so the pimps could see that the clients were interested in her more than in their working girls.

At the end of the third night, a couple of guys who worked for the organization approached her. The one who was older did all the talking.

"Hey you, pretty thing, what are you doing here all alone?"

"Me? Oh, I just love watching the girls. I admire them."

"Oh really? I never met anyone who admired whores." He looked at the other pimp, and they both laughed out loud. "I couldn't help but notice that you keep attracting lots of cars."

"Oh, I know. I get that all the time. It's very flattering, and I hate to decline all those hornies, but it's too dangerous for me to be getting into strangers' cars. Do you know what I mean?"

"Oh yes, we know what you mean; but, you are so gorgeous, don't you have a guy that can satisfy you?"

"Nope, I don't. No one can keep up with me. I have a super high sexual appetite. I want to fuck every single day. I love sex more than anything in the world, even more than the money! If I could fuck all night, I would do it for free."

Both pimps started to laugh even harder. They were amused by what they were hearing. To them, Natalia seemed very dumb, but that's what made her a perfect fit for that line of work. "So you just want to fuck but in a safe environment? Is that it?"

"Yup, that's all I want to do."

"Well, today is your lucky day. I am going to make you an offer you won't be able to resist. What if I told you that we could provide you with full protection and you can have all the sex you want for money or fun. That part is up to you."

"What? Are you for real? Oh, my God, I don't even need to think about it! I accept your offer. When can I start? I'm already horny."

"Smart choice, but first you have to go through an interview process. You will need to meet with our boss. We will tell him about you tonight, and you can meet him tomorrow."

"Perfect! I hope he is hot! I can show him a real interview!"

"Ok, horny girl, come to this address tomorrow at 8 p.m. Jason is our boss's name. Knock on the front door exactly three times and wear something sexy. We all think he is gay. He looks manly, but he hasn't fucked any of our girls yet. You do look like someone who can change his mind, though." The pimp smiled and handed Natalia a card with an address written on it.

"Thank you, boys; I will do my best. See you soon."

Natalia grabbed the next taxi passing by and headed home. The drivers usually dropped her off a couple of blocks away from her building, and she walked the rest of the way. All she wanted was for no one to follow her. Her role of being undercover had already started.

Natalia was happy with the progress she had made up to this point. It was undeniably disturbing to think what she was going to do tomorrow night; but at the same time, that was the only possible way to save little Nadia.

Destiny was just not giving the poor woman a break. Her struggles that started many years ago were nowhere near over. The only difference between Natalia at fourteen and her age at thirty-one was her strength to stand up for herself. She had guts to fight back and knowledge to do so.

The next day she spent the morning planning out her future steps. She practiced talking provocatively in front of the mirror and how to be seductive during her interview.

As a teenager, all of Natalia's sexual experiences were not voluntary. Now she had to act as if she were going into prostitution because she loved sex. That was entirely out of her comfort zone. She had to put her memories and fears aside.

Natalia hadn't had sex since she was eighteen years old. Even then it was at the maximum security prison, and it was rape that the Godmother and other inmates subjected her to. That could hardly be called sex by any means.

She had no clue how to show pimps and clients that she enjoyed sexual activities when in reality she did not. Natalia had to transform herself into an actress. She had to become a performer who was about to take center stage and give her best in the starring role.

In the afternoon, Natalia went to a clothing store where all the strippers loved to shop. It was easy to find something there. Natalia was a size two, and most of the clothes were a perfect fit. She knew she had to dress to impress.

Everything was ready to go hours ahead of schedule, but there was one little detail that Natalia still had to take care of: a picture of Nadia. She had to find a way somehow to have a mini version of Nadia's image with her.

It was evident that she couldn't just take the photo and keep it in her pocket. Anyone could find it and possibly recognize Nadia. Then Natalia's cover would be exposed and she as well as her daughter would be in danger.

Being not only beautiful but also smart, Natalia came up with a unique idea. She had a locket necklace with Nadia's mini picture already inside. She wore it for special occasions and that evening one was of those. Natalia couldn't just put it around her neck because it was a distinct locket. She decided to paint all over it with a black marker and bury it somewhere.

Natalia colored the locket and called for a taxi. When she got dropped off near the spot, she found a few tall trees that were surrounded by many thick bushes. It was not more than a hundred feet away from the location where she used to watch the girls while sitting on the bench.

Natalia quickly sat down on the ground next to one of the trees and when no one was around dug a small hole using her large mailbox keys. She then carefully placed the locket inside and covered it back up with soil. Natalia got up and hailed a taxi that took her back home. She did an excellent job of camouflaging the locket and the spot where she buried it.

Now, the most critical part was to pass the initial interview with the head pimp, Jason. Natalia had no idea if she was going to be hired on the spot and put to work the same night or if she was going to be able to come and go as she pleased. The regular working girls that the organization held captive slept in particular locations or at assigned rooms within brothels. Her situation was going to be little different, or so she hoped.

As the evening slowly approached and now the clock was nearing 7 p.m., Natalia finished her makeup and got dressed. She also packed a small shoulder bag with a couple of bras, underwear, and short tops, as well as a few skirts. She wasn't sure when she be back.

Natalia was going to hide the house keys inside of a small box mounted under the back-end of her car. She had installed that secret compartment a couple of years ago in case of an emergency. No one, other than she, knew about it. Plus, most of the residents at that property were wealthy and of high integrity.

By 7:15, Natalia was ready to go. Without reminiscing or

second-guessing her decision, she grabbed her stuff and walked to the parking garage. She successfully hid the house keys and walked out to the main road.

At the beginning of her walk, she didn't see that many cars but with every passing block, more and more of them started to appear. It was easy to notice Natalia walking on the sidewalk. Black fishnet stockings covered her legs. She was wearing high-heeled stilettos, a silver mini skirt, and a black tank top. Natalia decided not cover up with a jacket. She wanted to look as sexy as possible for the pimp, Jason.

Her beautiful hair was down, flowing in the wind every time she took a step. A couple of days back Natalia had added a few dirty-blond highlights to hair. She wanted to make herself stand out from the rest of the prostitutes. The usual hair color in that profession was either platinum blond or jet black. Plus, the new hairstyle made Natalia look more feminine and sensual.

As she continued walking block after block, more and more people in passing cars started to notice her. Many of them slowed down to stare at her eye-catching looks. Her beauty was hard to miss, even for those who see gorgeous women often, on TV or in real life. Something about the way she walked made her look very sexy, feminine and classy all at the same time. Even with the provocative outfit, she was wearing, Natalia looked like a model on the runway of a well-known fashion show.

When she got closer to the center of the city, she noticed a lot more people out on the streets. It was a mix of visitors, residents who were making their way home and just couples looking for a romantic place to eat. In some strange and confusing way Natalia still loved the city, and yet she hated it intensely at the same time. It was a mixed feeling that kept her balanced.

The address she was walking toward was in a surprisingly easily accessible location. It was behind one of the busiest strip clubs and only one block away from a tourist area where hundreds of vendors were selling souvenirs and gadgets. Natalia found it disturbing that the organization was operating so close to where so many families came to shop. She couldn't help but think that it was done on purpose, to make it easier for them to hide the young kidnapped girls.

When Natalia made it to the street where the building was, she realized that it was still a little too early. She decided to check out a few shops and took a detour through a side street. She felt fearless walking around those same streets where she used to work day and night, while scared and helpless.

The very first vendor on the strip caught her attention. It looked like he was selling only sunglasses. Natalia thought it was strange that he had just this one product, mainly since it was already dark outside. She didn't need any glasses, but the guy was also looking her way, so she decided to check it out.

As Natalia headed towards him, he smiled. In case she was going to pass right by he decided to shout. "Miss, miss, come here! You look way too beautiful and fragile! You need a little something to give you a fearless touch. Nice shades will bring out the bold look in you. The kind that female cops have! Come on! It's a dangerous world out there!"

Natalia, who only intended to walk by his stand, stopped and turned around. What he said somehow intrigued her. She wanted clarification on one of the points he made. "Did you just say that I look fragile? You mean I look weak and scared?"

"Yes, exactly. That's what I meant!" He laughed back.

"Really? Even my revealing outfit doesn't show that I'm not scared to be out and about or that I'm not fragile?"

"No, not really! It's Moscow. Many girls dress like you!"

"Hmmm. Ok, so you think that sunglasses can fix my appearance and make me look like I'm fearless? Is that it?"

"Yes, I do, and I have a perfect pair in mind for you."

"Oh, thanks, but I don't have money on me."

"It's ok. It's a present because you are beautiful!"

The guy turned around and pulled out a hard faux leather case from his inventory bag. He opened it up and took the sunglasses out. When Natalia saw them, she smiled in an amused manner. The glasses he was holding were black Aviators, the kind that was popular among male and female cops.

"Take them, they are yours. I only had one pair and for some reason didn't put these glasses out for sale with the rest of my inventory. Now I know why. These glasses are meant to be for you." said the guy and handed them and the box to Natalia.

She gently took the sunglasses out of his hand and put them on. The guy smiled and gave her a thumbs-up. Natalia thanked him and walked away. The moment she had them on she felt a strong feeling of empowerment. Now she knew why the guy wanted her to have them; it made total sense.

After Natalia walked the strip for a few more seconds, she realized that she had gotten carried away. She looked at her watch and saw the time. It was 7:55. Natalia became nervous and quickly got off the strip, taking the first side street. She didn't want to be late and started to walk much faster. A few minutes later Natalia ended up right in front of the place where she was supposed to be. She got there right on time.

The building looked clean and well-kept from the outside, but Natalia only imagined what was happening on the inside. She put on a fresh coat of bright, red lipstick and adjusted her tank top. Natalia was ready to go but anxious. The main door she was standing in front of was painted red which she thought was strange. To her, it was showing to the outsiders that either love or pain was happening behind it. Neither of the two was appealing.

Natalia carefully took a couple of steps up to the door and knocked on it precisely three times, just as the pimps told her to do. A moment later she heard footsteps coming towards the door. She went down one step and fixed up her hair. The lock turned, and with the metal chain still on, the door opened.

Natalia couldn't see who was behind it. The only thing she could see was darkness.

"Do you have an appointment?" asked a masculine voice. It sounded intimidating and yet in some strange way very calming.

"Hi, baby!" answered Natalia and took a step back up to the door, trying to show off her cleavage. "I am here to see Jason. He and I are going to have a fun interview. I'm going to show him how good I can fuck!" Natalia paused. She became uncomfortable and was afraid that she was overdoing her acting. On top of that, talking like that was out of her character.

"You are here to see Jason? Ok, but first I need to see you. Take off your Aviators! You look like you are here to make an arrest, not to fuck!" The man let out a short laugh but didn't say anything else.

Without overthinking, Natalia slightly pulled up her glasses and looked at the darkness behind the door. A moment later the man moved the chain, and the door opened a little more. Natalia couldn't yet see him, but there was just enough light to catch his silhouette. It looked intriguing and attractive, yet somehow forbidding.

A draft of air brought a scent from the hallway and out the door. Natalia involuntarily inhaled it. The smell was of that man's cologne. It was seductive and sensual. Strangely, it made her feel at ease and even aroused.

"So, you are here to see Jason. For what may I ask?"

"I am here because I'm applying for a job. I love the nightlife, the streets, the sex, and the money. I just want to have fun without endangering myself, and two guys that work for Jason told me that I would be a great fit. They said that he could provide me with the protection I need as long as I bring in lots of money. Is that guy Jason a big deal or is he not?"

Her sales pitch was perfect. The man got very captivated by the way Natalia presented herself. "You're asking me if Jason is all that? He is all that and more!" he answered in a little ticked-off manner. She didn't know if the way she talked was a good or bad sign, but she was hoping he liked what he heard.

A moment later the door opened all the way, and the man was standing in the doorway. He was now fully visible to Natalia, and she was surprised. She was stunned and confused by the way he looked. The guy who stood in front of her was the most handsome man she had ever seen. He looked like he was in his early 40s. His eyes were captivating. They looked like they were filled with frustrations but also with unusual kindness. He was wearing a perfectly pressed black suit and white shirt, unbuttoned at the neckline. The man was gorgeous in every possible way and very sexy on top of it.

At first Natalia's memory immediately took her back to that night when Madam Liz walked in with a man who was dressed just like that yet something was different. The man standing in front of her didn't look like a person who could kill. There was something very different about him, even in the way he was looking at her. It was unexplainable and almost scary.

The moment their eyes met, there was a silence between them and an awkwardness. Natalia was more than sure that they had never met before. The man didn't even have any familiar features yet there was something about him that made her feel connected.

His masculine body and broad shoulders gave out an impression of him being a protector. His kind but relentless stare was burning into her eyes in a captivating way. His cologne was arousing every fiber of her skin. His facial features and rugged build looked like a very talented artist had sculpted him. It didn't even matter that he looked like he hadn't shaved in a few days. His short facial hair made him look more manly and appealing to all of Natalia's senses.

She didn't know what to say or what to do. Her body was under the feeling that she had never felt before. It was loving, warm and even extraordinary. All that was turning into an uncontrollable sexual urge and desire that she had never experienced before. She had an intense need to feel the man's touch.

"Come in," he said with a gentle voice and moved away from the door, making room for her to walk in. They were still staring at each other, as Natalia slowly walked into the building.

Now, the darkness was all around her, but to her amazement, she wasn't scared. Natalia felt surprisingly comfortable and secure, unlike what she was expecting. When she was already in, she turned towards him. Even though the hallway was dark, the lights from the outside helped Natalia to see him better. She noticed that he had a genuine smile on his masculine face. "I am Jason. Are you ready to talk?"

Natalia's eyes opened wide, but she was still silent. She was acting like someone under hypnosis. She wasn't able to control her emotions or what she was feeling. Natalia didn't understand if what she was feeling was fear or if it was love at first sight, the kind of love that she saw in romantic movies.

The door slowly closed behind her, and she disappeared into the darkness of the corridor and the unknown.

COMING SOON – BOOK II

VERONIKA GASPARYAN

It Was A
TEST OF FAITH

Acknowledgments

The most heartfelt thanks are and always will go to the two people who inspired every single writing I created or will create in the future. Honorable appreciations go to them first as they are not with us any longer. The first is my grandfather, Sergey Movsesovitch Israelyan, who left me and this world twenty years ago. His physical body is gone, but he is always with me, protecting and watching over me like an angel. Thank you for being the only person in this world who loved me unconditionally from the day I was born and until your last breath. Thank you for inspiring me to fight through the hardships and never lose my faith. I still cry every time I mention your name, but I know that you are proud of me and one day we will celebrate our birthday together again. Another honorable thank you goes to my college professor of English, Richard J. Walton. He is also not with us since December of 2012, but he left a permanent impact on my faith and where my life path goes. Mr. Walton read my class papers many years back when they had dozens of mistakes and were written in half-broken English and still advised me that I have to become a writer and share my stories with the world. Loved by everyone, kind to all, and never forgotten by any, he will stay in my heart forever. RIP Mr. Walton. RIP grandpa.

A unique and endless thank you to the legendary Patricia Barnett – Transformational Leader, Bestselling Author, Creator of Results Mastery for Women and most importantly – a fantastic friend. Patricia, you have inspired me as well as thousands of people around the world to begin to dream again and to achieve those exact dreams. Your unmatched passion for serving others benefited me so much to move from the point of just hoping for a better life to the end of achieving the real success I so desired. You do the same for everyone who asks for your support. Thank you for being there for me and for your help in breaking through my barriers to accomplish positive results and in such a short time. Your *ELEVATE* program empowered me to create a level of freedom to live the rest of my life to the fullest. I am forever grateful to you for calibrating my vision and for helping me to find my real life's purpose. Thank you for countless hours you spent guiding me towards the light even when everything around me seemed so dark. Thank you for inspiring, empowering, and elevating me and many others to live a life of greater joy, expanded success and increased fulfillment. I am so happy and grateful knowing that you honestly see and want the best for me. I sincerely appreciate you from the depth of my heart.

Thank you to the special and the most patient lady I know - Mary Ring from Empower Your Writing. It's impressive to see how someone can be so kind and easy going and yet so focused and detail oriented. I am glad that we are working together, and thankful for your endless help day after day and week after week with proofreading and editing my work. Thank you for everything you have done for me so far and for all the time we will be spending together in the future.

A loving thank you to my oldest son, Daniel Ayriyan. You have shown me what a strong mind can do and how positive thinking can make all the difference. Thank you for being such a smart and talented young man and for making me proud in so many ways. Thank you for staying strong during the hardships our family has faced and for giving me the most terrific quote that I used when creating the dedication to this story. Love you to the moon and back and wish you to achieve everything you desire in life.

Another warm thank you goes to my youngest son, Rafael. I love you for being the most life-loving child I have ever met. You are so similar to me and yet much better in every way. Thank you for being understanding, during the many long days I worked on this story. Thank you for making me feel better when I was sad and needed to see love. Thank you for being you, and I wish that all of your dreams come true in the exact way you want them to happen.

A tranquil and positively charged thank you to my friend who kept me grounded and at peace as well as helped my family with body and soul alignment. Diane Lupo from Inner Voice Reiki kept my faith going and helped me to stay tuned to my desired destiny that awaits me in the nearest future. The Medium and Psychic Roxanne Jasparro gave me those small but very vital messages and signs from the dear people who are not with me any longer and for helping my son with his interests towards tranquility. Last but not least thanks to my good friend, Lisa Casinelli – the Reiki Master and Healer, who had provided me with amazingly positive energy and honest advice when it counted the most. I am grateful for your light and calm nature. Continue creating beauty around you and help those who need your healing powers.

Creative and exciting thank you to Zoella Rose Designs for designing the most beautiful and detailed cover I have ever seen. It's been pure pleasure to work with you. I cannot wait for us to collaborate hand and hand in creating even more amazing pieces of art. You are beyond talented. I'm confident I have never met anyone who didn't mind me sending hundreds of emails back and forth just for one part of the cover. Thank you!

Thanks to The Four Dames – Patricia Barnett, Julie Hamilton, Lynn Kitchen & Marilyn Macha, as well as Koby Benvenisti from Koby Ben Consulting for changing my mindset and rerouting my talents onto the path of my dreams. Thank you for the fantastic opportunity you gave me with the phenomenal Modern Day Millionaires Program and endless amount of support you provided during many months when it was needed most. A special thank you to Koby for putting together a once-in-a-lifetime event at Carnegie Hall in NYC in November of 2016. This program gathered together Bob Proctor, Les Brown and other top speakers in human potential and Laws of the Universe. Koby, because of your dream becoming a reality, my path crossed with you and the Dames and from that point my life has changed forever. Blessings to you all.

Also a special thank you goes to a few people who made an impact on me in one way or another, which in turn affected my writing of this book. First of all, thanks to my favorite cousin of all, Dr. Tigran Kazaryan who lives in Germany and who contributed some of the valuable information and material to this book. Secondly, thanks to Fezan Sayed, who was my boss for a few years in the past and who made the most significant impact on the way I write and how to use the beautiful English language. Thank you for teaching me how to pay attention to every detail and how to be a perfectionist when I want to relate my ideas to others through my writing. Last but not least, thanks to Patty Rathbun Pascetta, my friend, and my favorite reader. Thank you for being so passionate about my writing and for helping me dozens of times with questions I needed quick answers on during the creation of this book. I genuinely appreciate your help and dedication. My wish for you is always to be blessed.

The last and very heartfelt appreciation goes to those who were the voice of doubt. It was you who inspired me to rise above and go beyond my fears, limitations and what could have held me back. It was you who helped propel me forward to overcome obstacles that I had faced while writing this story month after month. Thank you for playing your part in helping me to see that indeed, ALL things are possible when you rise above it all.

ABOUT THE AUTHOR

Veronika Gasparyan was born in the beautiful city of Sochi, Russia in 1981 and is a proud descendant of many generations of Armenian ancestors on both sides of her family. Today she lives in Rhode Island, US, and is a published author with over 10 thousand copies of her memoir *Mother at Seven* sold from its release in July of 2016. From a very young age, Veronika enjoyed playing the piano which resulted in her attending a music school for ten years, and eventually the prestigious Sochi College of Arts and Music. Other than the music, Veronika has always displayed a profound love of reading, and at a very young age, read dozens of books from her grandfather's vast, personal library. Veronika is a strong believer in laws of attraction and positive thinking and is working on other books that she hopes will provide emotional support to those who are in need. She is especially hoping that her work can help those who have given up or have already lost their hope for better days and a joyful life

Mother
at Seven

The shocking
true story of
an Armenian girl's
stolen childhood
and her family's
unspeakable
cruel betrayal

VERONIKA GASPARYAN

www.ingramcontent.com/pod-product-compliance
Lightning Source LLC
Chambersburg PA
CBHW032039240626
47154CB00003B/992